"I'm enjoying this. Being with you. Knowing that you're a completely free woman and that I like you, and that just about anything could happen between us."

Kate puzzled over that. *Anything?*

"I just got out of a five-year engagement."

"I remember."

"I can't do this!" she said.

"Why not?"

"It was two days ago!"

"So?"

"I have to figure out what went wrong, to make sure it doesn't happen again."

"You know what happened, Kate," Ben claimed.

Only then did she realize that she was still sitting on his lap, in his car, in her driveway, for anyone to see! She let go of his shirt, pushed away from him and slid onto her own seat with every bit of dignity she could muster, which wasn't much.

Dear Reader,

Well, if there were ever a month that screamed for a good love story—make that six!—February would be it. So here are our Valentine's Day gifts to you from Silhouette Special Edition. Let's start with *The Road to Reunion* by Gina Wilkins, next up in her FAMILY FOUND series. When the beautiful daughter of the couple who raised him tries to get a taciturn cowboy to come home for a family reunion, Kyle Reeves is determined to turn her down. But try getting Molly Walker to take no for an answer! In Marie Ferrarella's *Husbands and Other Strangers,* a woman in a boating accident finds her head injury left her with no permanent effects—except for the fact that she can't seem to recall her husband. In the next installment of our FAMILY BUSINESS continuity, *The Boss and Miss Baxter* by Wendy Warren, an unemployed single mother is offered a job—not to mention a place to live for her and her children—with the grumpy, if gorgeous, man who fired her!

"Who's Your Daddy?" is a question that takes on new meaning when a young woman learns that a rock star is her biological father, that her mother is really in love with his brother—and that she herself can't resist her new father's protégé. Read all about it in *It Runs in the Family* by Patricia Kay, the second in her CALLIE'S CORNER CAFÉ miniseries. *Vermont Valentine,* the conclusion to Kristin Hardy's HOLIDAY HEARTS miniseries, tells the story of the last single Trask brother, Jacob—he's been alone for thirty-six years. But that's about to change, courtesy of the beautiful scientist now doing research on his property. And in Teresa Hill's *A Little Bit Engaged,* a woman who's been a bride-to-be for five years yet never saw fit to actually set a wedding date finds true love where she least expects it—with a pastor.

So keep warm, stay romantic, and we'll see you next month....

Gail Chasan
Senior Editor

Please address questions and book requests to:
Silhouette Reader Service
U.S.: 3010 Walden Ave., P.O. Box 1325, Buffalo, NY 14269
Canadian: P.O. Box 609, Fort Erie, Ont. L2A 5X3

A LITTLE BIT ENGAGED

TERESA HILL

Silhouette®

SPECIAL EDITION®

Published by Silhouette Books

America's Publisher of Contemporary Romance

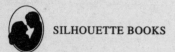

SILHOUETTE BOOKS

ISBN 0-373-24740-0

A LITTLE BIT ENGAGED

Copyright © 2006 by Teresa Hill

Visit Silhouette Books at www.eHarlequin.com

Printed in U.S.A.

Books by Teresa Hill (under the name Sally Tyler Hayes)

Silhouette Special Edition

Magic in a Jelly Jar #1390
*Heard It Through the Grapevine #1546
A Little Bit Engaged #1740

Silhouette Intimate Moments

Whose Child is This? #439
Dixon's Bluff #485
Days Gone By #549
Not His Wife #611
Our Child? #671
Homecoming #700
Temporary Family #738
Second Father #753
Wife, Mother…Lover? #818
†Dangerous To Love #903
†Spies, Lies and Lovers #940
†Cinderella and the Spy #1001
†Her Secret Guardian #1012

*under the name of Teresa Hill
†Division One

TERESA HILL

lives in South Carolina with her husband, son and daughter. A former journalist for a South Carolina newspaper, she fondly remembers that her decision to write and explore the frontiers of romance came at about the same time she discovered, in junior high, that she'd never be able to join the crew of the *Starship Enterprise*.

Happy and proud to be a stay-home mom, she is thrilled to be living her lifelong dream of writing romances.

To everyone at St. Mary's.

I'm positive it wasn't that long ago that I sent my son to kindergarten in his little blue dress pants and white polo shirt. I remember so clearly thinking I'd have a child at St. Mary's forever. And yet, somehow, this is our last year. My daughter's graduating from the eighth grade this spring. Somehow, twelve years have gone by.

Thanks for all you do, for all your hard work, for all the memories.

Chapter One

"So, have you and Joe set a wedding date yet?"

Kate Cassidy barely managed not to choke on her carrot-stick appetizer.

Trapped in the corner by an interior designer, she swallowed hard and relaxed her facial muscles in hopes of avoiding that really unattractive expression she wore when she just wanted to scream.

It was truly an unattractive look.

Kate knew because she'd looked in the mirror one day while she made it, hoping it wouldn't be that bad. But it was. She'd vowed to eradicate the expression from her face, but it was hard. Especially lately, when someone asked *that* question. Third time this evening at the Board of Realtors dinner, in fact.

"Not yet," she said quietly, with what she hoped was a bit of a smile.

"Oh." The woman, Gloria someone, waited expectantly for Kate to elaborate, which Kate wasn't going to do. She'd learned that if she was silent long enough, most people quit asking and went away. But Gloria wasn't budging.

Okay. If things got really bad, she could always sink so low as to play the sympathy card. *Sorry, Mom.* She let her expression fall, allowed a shimmer of tears to come into her eyes.

"Oh, I'm sorry, Kate. I guess it's just too soon, huh?"

Kate nodded with what she hoped was appropriate sadness and grief, hoping her mother would understand. Kate had finally found something she didn't know how to handle. All her plans that had always gone so well seemed to have fallen apart, and she didn't know what was right anymore or what to do. It had started with her mother's death and spilled over into every aspect of her life.

"It just takes time," Gloria said kindly, making Kate feel worse. "And Joe's such a sweetie. I'm sure he understands."

Kate wasn't so sure he did. And she didn't want to think about it. She wanted to ignore the whole mess and hope it went away or solved itself, or that the answer just dropped out of the sky or something.

Vaguely aware of new voices around her, Kate looked up to see Charlie Sims, president of the Magnolia Falls, Georgia, Board of Realtors.

"Kate, how are you?" he asked, extending a hand.

"Great, Charlie. How are you?"

"Couldn't be better, my dear. Have you met my wife, Charlotte?"

"No, I haven't." Kate smiled down at the pint-size blonde on Charlie's arm.

Charlie introduced them, and then Charlotte

launched into a tale about their recent wedding. Kate didn't listen. She was too busy planning her escape. Was there anyone in this room who didn't know that she and Joe were supposed to have married this summer but hadn't because Kate's mother's cancer had come back and she'd died in the spring?

There. Kate spotted two absolute strangers in the corner. She was ready to make her excuses when Gloria said, "Oh, that sounds like fun. I'd love to do that."

"Fabulous," Charlie said, sounding genuinely appreciative.

That got Kate's attention. She wanted Charlie to be happy with her, because there wasn't a real estate agent in town Charlie didn't know. He was a veritable gold mine of referrals for Kate's fledgling mortgage company.

"What about you, Kate?" Charlie's wife asked. "Care to come join us?"

Kate stood there with her mouth open. She had no idea what she'd just been asked to do, but if Gloria could do it, surely Kate could, too. Anything for Charlie and his referrals.

"Of course," Kate said. "Sounds like fun."

"Oh, it is. The kids are great," Charlie's wife said.

Kids? They were doing something with kids?

"If you two will give me your fax numbers, I'll send you an application. Fax it back, and we'll match you up."

Kate wasn't sure if she'd just applied for a job or joined a dating service. Match us up? No, that couldn't be right. Everyone here wanted news of her upcoming wedding to Joe. Plus this was something to do with kids. It couldn't be dating.

Kate obediently gave Charlie's wife her fax number.

It wasn't until the next day, when the fax arrived, that she vaguely remembered something about Charlie's new wife taking over as director of the Big Brothers/Big Sisters Program, and that Kate had just volunteered to be a Big Sister.

Okay. How hard could that be?

Maybe she'd get lucky, and her little sister would be one of the few people in town who wouldn't question her about why she and Joe hadn't gotten married yet.

Ben Taylor hovered at the end of the hallway leading to the front door, assessing his chances of sneaking out of his office without getting caught, and thereby avoiding a lecture from his nearly eighty-year-old secretary.

Her long-distance vision wasn't good, and she hated her bifocals. Ben figured the odds were at least three-to-one against her noticing him leaving. Which meant he could put off for now her lecture about his unfortunate tendencies to wander about, loose in the community, doing his freelance, do-gooder thing and getting into trouble, all while just trying to help people.

Ben really tried to help. He wasn't sure if he was just bad at it or if people's problems were getting worse. It seemed no one walked in with a simple issue he could solve anymore, and really, wasn't he here to solve problems?

"Should have just kidnapped the girl," he muttered to himself. "Or maybe held her hostage until I could talk some sense into her."

"You say something, Pastor?" It was Rose, the nice lady who lived three blocks down and came to clean every other day.

"No, ma'am." Ben sighed. "But I'm going out for

a few minutes. Will you tell Mrs. Ryan if she asks about me?"

"Sneakin' off again, Pastor?"

"Maybe," he admitted.

He and Mrs. Ryan would have to come to an understanding about his straying from the office one of these days, but this wasn't the day, and he wasn't up to a scolding by a scrunched-over, outspoken taskmaster who reminded him of his great-grandmother.

"Will you tell her I've gone out?" he asked Rose.

"I guess I'll have to," Rose said. "I'm the only one who's not scared of her."

"I'm not scared," he claimed. It was just that... Well, she did look a lot like his great-grandmother, and he'd been raised to believe a boy never, ever argued with his great-grandmother. His father would have seen it as an appalling lack of respect. Of course, his father would have thought sneaking out like this was cowardly, which made this a classic no-win situation. He'd take the cowardly way again. Rose wished him luck and said he owed her one. He decided he'd bring her a latte from that little shop down the block. She loved them but considered them a luxury. It was the least he could do for her for saving him from Mrs. Ryan.

He was nearly to the door when Rose said, "Now, just to be clear on this, you're not really going to kidnap anyone, are you?"

"No. Promise." The church probably frowned upon kidnapping and hostage taking. He'd just have to find another way. He was supposed to be able to keep people here long enough to help them without resorting to those tactics, even if a kidnapping could have made things so much simpler.

He must be doing something really wrong.

"Okay," Rose said. "I just wouldn't want to be around if Mrs. Ryan got wind of you kidnapping someone."

"Neither would I." He would really be scared of the woman then.

"So," Rose said. "What should I tell her when she comes looking for you?"

"Nothing…"

"Pastor—"

"Okay, if she threatens to pull out your fingernails one by one, you can tell her I've gone to see Charlotte Sims at the Big Brothers/Big Sisters office. But only under threat of torture. Understand?"

"Of course."

"Thanks, Rose."

He slipped out the door of the massive stone church, built seventy-five years before, and tried not to think of his shortcomings as an Episcopalian priest, as Mrs. Ryan saw them. He was too young, wasn't married and had no children, so he obviously didn't know enough about life to help people with real problems. He tended to be more informal in how he related to his parishioners and how they related to him, than Mrs. Ryan thought was proper. She thought it scandalous that he asked people to call him Ben—Pastor Ben if they really felt it was necessary to add some title to his name. And he was always behind on his paperwork.

Those were his main failings, all of which he tried not to think about as he headed for Magnolia Falls' Main Street. He'd cross that and then go four blocks over, to Vine, to see Charlotte Sims, a woman he hoped would be more successful than he'd been at helping the teenager who'd shown up at his church yesterday morning but run away before Ben could do anything for her.

Honestly, she'd hardly given him ten minutes.

Was he really supposed to turn her life around in ten minutes?

Not that he'd left it at that.

He'd followed her, was probably lucky he hadn't been arrested for stalking. Mrs. Ryan would have loved that. The day that woman had to bail him out of jail was the day he was out of here for good. Defrocked. Wasn't that what they called it? He thought it sounded like an odd, modern-dance number or maybe some obscure cooking term.

Defrock the basted chicken pieces, and heat oven to 375....

Okay, so he'd like to avoid defrocking, kidnapping, hostage taking and stalking charges. He'd like to actually do some good. He'd like to feel useful. He'd like to not be afraid of Mrs. Ryan. He was her boss, after all. Not that she showed any understanding of that.

He grinned remembering how horrified his secretary had been by the girl's appearance yesterday. Truth be told, Ben had been a bit taken aback, as well.

She had badly dyed, jet-black hair that looked like she'd taken a razorblade to it, then gelled it to get it to stand up in every direction; she was wearing at least seven earrings. He didn't even want to imagine what else she might have pierced. Shannon wore a black leather jacket and tall boots, that odd white makeup on her face and nearly black lipstick.

And it wasn't even Halloween.

She looked as if she was twelve going on forty, but he'd found out she was actually fifteen, had lost her mother and the grandmother who'd raised her, and was now living with a father who couldn't have cared less about her, at least not as she told the story. She said straight-out that she didn't believe in God but was desperate enough that day to give God—well, actually Ben—a chance. Ten minutes to either help her or convince her to stay, neither of which he'd done.

And she was pregnant, which made the whole situation even more dire.

Ben had followed her, successfully avoided stalking charges, resisted kidnapping her, and found her in the parking lot of the local high school talking to one of his parishioners, Betty Williams, who happened to teach there. A nicer, more successful do-gooder, he'd never met. And Betty had told him to get Shannon into the local Big Brothers/Big Sisters program, if he could. They were full, with a waiting list a mile long. Betty had checked.

It had taken a little unauthorized deal making to get Shannon a spot at the front of the line, and he hated to make other kids wait longer for help, but there was the baby to consider. So Ben had turned wheeler-dealer, offering an as-yet-undefined favor to the director of Big Brothers/Big Sisters, which was why he was sneaking out of church this morning, to see what the deal would cost him.

He arrived at the pretty brick building and was just about to grab the door, when it opened on its own.

Hmm.

He liked open doors.

He thought they were a sign that someone was doing something right.

He was just about to walk through that open door when a tiny, curly-headed girl came barreling out. Afraid she was going to charge out of the building and right into the street, he yelled, "Hey, wait!"

She stopped, standing with her back to the door, not

trying to escape but holding the door open and gazing up at him with a puzzled smile.

"Oh," he said. "I thought you were taking off."

"Not by myself. I'm only six," she said, as if he had the IQ of a tomato. *Maybe one that had been defrocked along with the chicken?*

"Well...good," he said, bested by a six-year-old. "I tell you what. The door looks heavy. How 'bout I hold it?"

She shrugged, then grinned. Once he had the door, she did a little dance step and spun around. "Know what? I'm gonna be a dancer when I get big."

"Great."

She did another little twirl step right there in the hallway, and the little red ribbon that had been dangling from the end of one curl floated to the floor.

"Allie, wait," a woman inside called out.

Ben looked up to see a woman sitting just inside the door. She had her hands full, a baby cradled against her shoulder and a toddler missing a shoe whom she'd managed to catch by the hood of his jacket.

"You don't want to leave your mom," Ben said, moving to put his body between hers and the hallway, in case she decided to run for it.

"She's not my mom," Allie said. "She's my cousin. My mommy left, and her cousin has a little baby and a not-so-little one, and she's trying to take care of me, too. Only, we're a handful. I'm here to get a big sister. What about you?"

"I think I'm too old for them to give me a big brother. What do you think?"

She giggled. "You're really old."

"And you lost your hair ribbon," he said. "Let me get it."

Ben got down on his knees beside her, happy to

have a problem he could solve for a change. He grabbed the ribbon, then didn't quite know what to do with it. She really had a mountain of hair, and it was sticking out every which way. He wasn't sure what he could accomplish by way of subduing it with one ribbon. Was it for show, or did it have a real purpose?

"Looks like you two need some help," a nice, soft, feminine voice said.

Ben glanced to his right and saw legs, really nice legs. He looked up and saw a pretty blonde in a no-nonsense, dark-brown suit and a crisp white blouse. There was a brown satchel in her hand and an I-can-fix-this look on her face.

Okay, so he couldn't even get the hair ribbon thing right. Maybe it really wasn't his day. Maybe he shouldn't be out loose on the streets like this, even if he hadn't committed any crimes yet.

"This is my friend, Allie," he told the pretty blonde. "She's lost her ribbon."

"Again," Allie added.

"Again? Oh. Well, let's see if we can get it to stay in your hair." The woman put down her satchel and took the ribbon in hand, working what looked like magic with the girl's unruly hair in a matter of minutes with nothing but her two hands, and then secured the ribbon. "Double knot and tight. That's the key to keeping a hair ribbon in place."

"Really?" Allie bounced up and down and then stared out of the corner of her eyes, trying to find the ribbon.

"It's still there," Ben told Allie, then let himself look at the woman again. She knew how to fix ribbons and hair, and she was kind as well. Seemed like she liked children, too. He wondered how she knew about the double-knotted-ribbon thing. "Thank you."

"You're welcome. She's adorable."

"Oh...she's not mine," Ben said, happy to have an excuse to clear that up, just in case. "I'm just the official door holder."

"I'm here to get a big sister," Allie said. "Are you gonna get a little sister?"

Good girl, Ben thought, altogether pleased with the turn of events.

He'd let Allie interrogate the pretty blonde, and then maybe he could casually work into the conversation the fact that he had no wife and no children and then... Who knew? He might even get a lunch date out of the deal.

Ben couldn't remember the last time he had a date.

He checked to see if he had his clerical collar on, then remembered he didn't. Mrs. Ryan, with a very disapproving look, had reminded him of that this morning, but he'd gotten distracted and hadn't put it on.

Okay. This was not a bad thing.

The collar made people uncomfortable.

Especially women.

Not that he was all that good with women even without the collar.

"I already have two little sisters," the woman said. "Real sisters, I mean. But you can't have too many little sisters, right?" She looked at Ben.

"Right," he said. Could he interest her in a pregnant fifteen-year-old?

"So I came to get another one," the woman said.

"Oh, good. I pick you," Allie said, then turned and yelled back into the office. "Miss Grace? I found one all by myself! See?"

In the waiting room, a woman kneeling at the feet of the now completely shoeless toddler looked up and sighed. The little boy was trying to wiggle his way off the chair. A second woman was holding the baby, who was sucking on his fists.

"Allie, Miss Charlotte will find you a big sister. You can't just grab one in the hallway." Miss Grace grabbed the toddler by his left ankle, which kept him from sliding out of the chair, but he howled in protest. To top it all off, the baby started crying. The poor mother looked as though she might sit down and cry, too.

Ben had seen that exhausted-mother look before and stepped in. "Ma'am, would it be okay if I walked you and Allie and the boys to your car?"

She gave him a look that said she would have kissed his feet, if need be, to get help to the car with Allie and the two squirmy, crying boys. Allie came to his side and put her hand trustingly in his. Miss Grace handed him the toddler, whom he held against his shoulder.

"Thank you so much. I'll get the shoes, the baby and the diaper bag—"

"I've got the diaper bag," said the pretty blonde who was a whiz with ribbons.

Ben, this might be your lucky day.

If he could just get her phone number. And find the time to have lunch or something, and if she was willing… If he could sneak away from Mrs. Ryan for a few more hours, and if this woman actually liked him and wanted to see him again, he might manage to have a life outside the church.

People said he needed one. They warned about getting completely caught up in his work and forgetting to have a personal life.

Ben held the toddler, who was studying him with distrusting eyes. Grace had the baby. The blonde had the diaper bag. Allie was close by. They were ready.

"Thank you both so much," Grace said.

"We're having one of those days." Allie sounded six going on twenty-six.

After a few more moments of confusion over misplaced car keys, a lost sock and a small battle of wills with the toddler over his car seat, the little blue station wagon was loaded up and on its way, leaving Ben alone with the blonde and trying to remember how to flirt. He'd never been that good at it, and for the past few years, he hadn't had time, even if he did remember how.

She saved him by sticking out her hand and saying, "Sorry. It was so hectic back there, I didn't have time to introduce myself. I'm Kate Cassidy."

He took her hand in his. "Hi. Ben Taylor."

"Nice to meet you. Are you going back to the office, too?"

"Yes."

They turned and walked together.

Kate said, "So, are you a big brother?"

"No, I'm in the highly precarious position of owing the director a favor, and I'm not sure yet how she's going to collect. I hear she can be brutal. I could have six little brothers by lunchtime."

"Charlotte does seem to know how to take advantage of every opportunity."

"She twisted your arm, too?"

"No. I can't say that. It was more like…" They'd gotten back to the office door, and Ben held the door open for her. Kate nodded in the direction of his hand. "…like opening a door in front of me and knowing I'd walk right through it. You know what I mean?"

"Oh, yeah. Those get me every time," he said, thinking the door metaphor could really be a sign. He believed in signs. And phone numbers. He had to get her phone number before she disappeared. He was trying to picture his calendar through the end of the week, to see if he had a day open for lunch, when they walked into the Big Brothers/Big Sisters office one more time.

"Kate," the receptionist said. "It's so good to see you. I've been waiting to see an announcement in the paper, but I must have missed it. You and Joe have picked a wedding date, haven't you?"

Ben barely managed not to growl.

Chapter Two

"Not yet," Kate told the woman, whose nameplate read Melanie Mann.

Was it Ben's imagination or did she seem upset by the question? Ben stood behind her, eavesdropping shamelessly.

"Oh. Well, I understand," her friend said. "No time to plan, right?"

"Right," Kate agreed. "Not yet."

Ben thought if she really wanted to marry this man, surely she could find time to plan a wedding.

"Sorry about your mom," Melanie said. "I know you must miss her terribly."

"Yes, I do," Kate said.

Okay, so he was a cad. A truly terrible person. It sounded as if she'd lost her mother recently, and here he was, hoping there was something wrong between her and her fiancé, just so Ben could maybe have lunch with her.

He sighed, then frowned, then found both women looking at him.

"Sorry we were so rude," Kate said.

"No. It's not that. I was just thinking of…a problem I need to address." His own shortcomings.

"Melanie and I went to high school together," Kate said. "This is Melanie Mann. Melanie, this is Ben Taylor."

Melanie picked up a tiny, yellow Post-it note. "Ahhh. That explains it. Charlotte just handed me a scribbled note that I think says, 'Ben, ten-thirty, today.'" She turned to Ben, "That would be you?"

"That's me." He held out a hand. "Nice to meet you."

"You, too. But I'm afraid we have a problem. Charlotte didn't check with me before scheduling a time for you to come in, and she already has a ten-thirty appointment. With Kate."

"It's all right. I can wait," Ben offered. He was already in hot water with Mrs. Ryan. Another few minutes away from the office wouldn't matter. "Besides, I just called this morning. I'm betting Kate's had an appointment longer than that. She looks like the organized type."

"Oh, definitely," Melanie said.

Kate hesitated, then said, "You don't have to be somewhere?"

"My morning's clear." So was lunch. Too bad he couldn't ask her. Not if she had a fiancé.

"Well, if you're sure, I do need to go ahead. I have paperwork to look over and a lunch meeting and three clients coming in this afternoon."

"Go ahead," Ben said, noting she'd said lunch *meet-ing*, not lunch *date*.

No lunch date. No wedding date. Still, none of his business.

Then he remembered she'd said she had two sisters. Maybe one of them would have lunch with him. If that didn't work out, maybe he could start a singles group at church....

Just so you can get a date, Ben?

Okay, he was sleep deprived from sitting up late into the night with a distraught couple while their baby had emergency surgery, and he was getting a little silly now, thinking to solve his non-social-life problem in one single morning out on the town. It wasn't as if the issue was urgent. He'd been here this long and not done a thing about it. The issue would still be there next week, next month, probably next year.

He really hoped he didn't wait until next year to do something about this.

Kate was giving him a funny look. So was Melanie.

"Sorry." He yawned deeply, unable to hold back the motion at all, and then said, "I can be easily distracted, and I was out way too late last night."

Which made it sound as though he was partaking in some blatantly unministerly things. "Working," he added. "I was working."

"Me, too," Kate said, giving him a puzzled look. "But I wouldn't have pictured you as the workaholic type."

"Which means what? That you are?"

"Well..." Kate hesitated.

"She most definitely is," Melanie said.

"What do you do?" Ben asked.

"Kate has her own mortgage brokerage company.

She's the youngest person in our class to own her own business," Melanie said, sounding proud.

"It's not much," Kate claimed. "Me, a desk, a phone, a fax, a computer and an assistant. That's it."

"Still, it's all yours. I wish I had the guts to start something like that and make it work," Melanie said.

"It wasn't guts," Kate said. "You know how I like to do things my own way. Starting the business was the only way I could earn a living and not have someone else telling me what to do all the time."

She laughed when she said it, but Ben thought he must be right. A well-organized, ambitious workaholic who couldn't find time to plan her own wedding?

Not for him at all.

So why had he taken such an instant liking to her? Why did he feel as if someone had just opened a door and he wanted to walk through it?

The phone on Melanie's desk rang. She excused herself and picked it up. Ben and Kate took seats in the small waiting room and smiled politely at each other. He tried to think of a way to bring up the fiancé thing without being too obvious and then gave up on the obvious part.

"So," he said, because he felt the need to have it drilled into his head, "you're engaged?"

A pained look crossed her face. She hesitated way too long over her answer, then said weakly, "Yes."

That was interesting.

"Sorry." Ben frowned. "I'm being nosy, but… you don't sound too sure about that."

"No… I mean…" She frowned, too. "Honestly, I don't know what I mean."

He didn't know whether to feel guilty or happy. He really did try to do the right thing. He didn't succeed all the time, but he felt it was important to try.

So what was the right thing here?

She certainly shouldn't marry the guy if she did't love him....

They looked at each other again, her waiting to see what he said, him not knowing what to say but wanting to know more.

"Want to tell me about it?" he tried. He'd had a lot of success with that particular phrase. A lot of times people thought about it and decided they wanted to talk, and there he'd be. Maybe she wanted to talk.

"Maybe," she said, frowning. "Maybe it would be easier with a stranger. I mean, if I just brought up the idea that Joe and I might not get married to one of my siblings, all three of them would hear about it within seconds, and they'd have questions that I just couldn't answer, because...I don't know what to do, and I hate that. Don't you hate not knowing what to do?"

"I find myself quite often not knowing what to do," he admitted. Like now. Right now. What did he do now?

"But don't you hate it?"

"I don't like it, but...I guess I just think that's mostly what life is—stumbling along, not knowing what's going to happen, a lot of times not knowing what I should do but hoping I can figure out the right thing to do."

"It's awful. Life should be simpler," she argued. "We should always know what we should do. We should always be able to figure it out."

"And you can't figure out what to do now?"

"No," she complained. "Honestly, I'm not even sure if I'm engaged anymore. The date when we were supposed to be married has come and gone, and we're not married, and neither one of us has said a word about rescheduling. We just kind of... left things up in the air. Which is really not like me. But I just don't know what to do. If I did, I'd do it. But I don't, so I haven't done anything, and I'm really not good in situations like this." She frowned again. "You know?"

"I think so," he said, thinking that if she didn't even know if she was engaged anymore, who did? Thinking that a good next question would be, *Do you love this man? Does he love you?* When what he wanted to say was, *If you weren't engaged, would you give me your phone number?*

He blamed the impulse, again, on lack of sleep and acute loneliness. Apparently, he was in worse shape than he thought.

"You're very easy to talk to," she said, as if she didn't quite understand why.

He shrugged easily. "Years of training. I guess some of it took. And in my entirely professional opinion, I can tell you that most people get confused on a regular basis. It's perfectly normal."

Kate frowned. "And then they just don't do anything, because they're afraid they'll do the wrong thing? Or because they think maybe something will happen at some point, and then they'll just know what they're supposed to do?"

"Exactly."

"I hate that, too," she said. "I mean, how can we expect to get where we want to go, without figuring out what we want and making a plan for getting it?"

"So, you don't know what you want?" he asked cautiously, thinking he knew exactly what she was like. Tough on herself. Focused. Driven. Ambitious. Baffled by how difficult some people found life.

Obviously, she needed help. And it was possible he was helping her clarify her feelings. That was good, right?

"Maybe." She looked even more troubled and,

sounding doubtful said, "But this is supposed to be for the rest of my life. This is not a decision to mess up."

"No, it's not," he said, striving for an absolutely objective tone. One should be absolutely sure when choosing someone to marry. He'd give that advice to anyone who asked. Not just possibly engaged women he wanted to date.

"Maybe it's just cold feet," she suggested.

"Maybe," he agreed. He could be really good at this objective stuff.

"But it would be awful to lose the right man, just because I'm nervous about making that commitment or waiting for…well…"

Oh, yeah. What did she want from this relationship that was missing? What could he possibly say that would be unbiased here?

She just looked sad then. "I don't know what I want."

"I think you do," he said, then could have kicked himself.

Still, not bad advice, he told himself.

He'd learned from experience. People knew. They just didn't want to admit to themselves that they knew, because then they'd have to do something about it. If they could just pretend that they didn't know, they didn't have to do anything.

"Tell me what to do?" she asked.

"I can't. You're the only one who knows how you really feel." Then, because he felt guilty, he added, "Kate, if you really don't know, it's okay to let things ride for a little while until you figure it out. That's just being careful."

"I don't think I'm being careful. I think I'm being a coward."

If she'd been anyone else, he would have reached

over and squeezed her hand or patted her shoulder to try to comfort her because she looked so troubled. But Ben wasn't touching her.

"You think I'm awful, don't you?" she asked.

"No."

"You say that, but you sound like you think I'm awful. You're looking at me like you think I'm awful. Do you know Joe?"

"No."

"He's a good man. A very good man."

But that didn't make him right for her.

He groaned. Ben, gag yourself now. Right now.

If he had a needle and thread, he'd have sewn his mouth shut and known he deserved the pain it caused him.

"Now you look angry," she said.

"At myself. Not you."

"Why?"

"Because I'm wishing you weren't engaged," he admitted. "Which means I have no right giving you advice about this, and I have to shut up. Now."

She looked puzzled. "You mean…you want to… you and me?"

He nodded.

"Oh." Her mouth fell open and her eyes got big and round. Soft color filled her cheeks, and he started laughing, couldn't help it.

Either he was a terrible flirt or she was completely oblivious to him as a man, because it was obvious it hadn't even occurred to her that he might be interested in her. He either really liked her for that or felt sorry for himself for being invisible to her.

"I'm really not very good at this sort of thing," she said. "You know, the man-woman thing."

"Me, neither." Ben laughed some more. "Obviously."

"No. It's not you. It's me. If there was a textbook or a class in college or a test, I could have aced it. But there aren't any of those things when it comes to relationships. I mean, there are tons of books but they all say different things. Have you ever tried to make sense of all the different things written about relationships?"

"No."

"It's awful. Give me numbers. I can add them up. They always come up to the same thing. I love that about numbers. Ask me something about love, and I'm just baffled. You can't quantify it in any way. There's no definitive test for it. There's no checklist. It has an infinite number of variables. You can't even define the term. It means so many different things to people."

"It is annoying in those ways," he agreed.

She groaned aloud. "What am I going to do?"

"You'll figure it out," he said.

She stared at him and frowned. "You're a really nice man."

"And that's a bad thing?"

"No, it's not. It's just…I don't know what to do."

"And you're the only one who can decide."

She looked hopeless then, like she might cry sometime soon.

He stiffened his spine, tried to strengthen his resolve. He had to get away from her. Nothing else would save him.

"Okay. I'll stop talking now and go sit on the other side of the room, in case I'm tempted to do more harm than I've already done. It was nice to meet you, Kate. You'll do the right thing, whatever it is."

"I'm not so sure of that." She looked as if she might

cry at any minute. "I'm not very sure of anything right now."

Oh, great. Make her cry. Way to go, Ben.

"Kate, sorry to have kept you waiting," Charlotte Sims said, saving him from whatever he might have said by choosing that moment to walk into the reception area and place herself directly in front of him and Kate.

Kate looked panicked and guilty. Very guilty.

Ben finally noticed that her friend, Melanie, was staring at them both with rapt attention.

Charlotte looked puzzled. "Something wrong?"

"No," Ben said. "Not at all."

Things were right. Very right. She had saved him from saying something he would definitely regret and stepping across a line he had no right to cross.

"And it seems I've double booked myself. Again," Charlotte said, still studying all three people in the reception area to see what she'd missed.

"No problem," Ben said. "Kate can go first."

"You're sure?" she asked.

"Positive," he said, thinking, *Please, just go.*

"We won't be long," Charlotte assured him.

Kate stood up and followed the woman, turning briefly to shoot a puzzled look at Ben that he couldn't begin to decipher.

Was she mad at him?

He was mad at himself.

And too curious for his own good.

"Well," Melanie said. "That was interesting. How do you two know each other?"

"We don't," Ben insisted. "We just met at the front door to your office five minutes ago."

"Oh." She sounded terribly disappointed.

He wondered if he could ask her not to say anything about this to anyone, particularly Kate's kind-of-fiancé, but that would probably make them look even more guilty. He wondered if Melanie liked to gossip and how well she knew Joe, whom Kate might or might not love. He'd feel really guilty if the talk he and Kate had had had caused any trouble between her and her fiancé.

Ben, you should have slept in today, maybe not gotten out of bed at all. But Mrs. Ryan would have been horrified, and someone had to do the morning prayer service. Staying in bed really wasn't an option.

Keeping his mouth shut with Kate and staying out of her relationship with Joe…now, that was an option. He clamped his mouth shut, glanced at Melanie, only to find her grinning at him and staring right back.

"So," Melanie said. "Want to know about Kate and Joe?"

"No."

"Liar."

He bit his tongue and sat there, stone-faced. Now, she had him lying. Him…a minister.

But, if he'd told the truth, Melanie would have told him all about Kate and Joe, and it was definitely none of his business.

No way to win this one, Ben.

Melanie laughed at him and told him anyway. "They've been together forever. Five years now, I think."

Which could mean anything. That they were perfectly suited for each other or that they'd simply let things run on, with no inclination to take that final step, because they simply had no desire to actually be married.

"Supposed to get married this summer, but Kate's mom's cancer came back in the middle of planning the wedding, and then she died this spring, and... Well, I'm not sure what's going on now."

"Melanie—"

"But Joe really is a great guy."

So he'd heard.

"Still, you'd think if they were going to get married, they'd have done it by now," Melanie proclaimed.

Please, please, please, please, please, Ben begged silently. *Get me out of this. I'll be good. I promise.*

He closed his eyes, closed his ears as best he could, refusing to listen anymore. Melanie got a phone call, thank God, and then another one. She hadn't said one more word about Kate and Joe.

Charlotte Sims's office door opened, finally, and she and Kate came out. Ben stood up, thinking he would slide on into Charlotte's office and not have to say anything but a polite goodbye to Kate, and he'd have escaped relatively unscathed.

But then Melanie, who'd been on the phone again, put it down and said, "Hey, wait a minute. There's a really annoyed older woman on the phone who's lost a priest named Ben Taylor." She glared at him, looking at him like he was a snake. "Are you a priest?"

Kate's head whirled around, and she stood there, openmouthed, waiting for him to answer. Charlotte Sims was staring, too.

"It's not what you think," he said.

Melanie held out the phone. "Pastor? If this is you, it's your secretary. She's saying something about you slipping past her and going AWOL." Then she said into the phone, "He's not dangerous is he?"

Ben groaned and took the phone, hoping Mrs. Ryan

had the courtesy to say that no, he was not dangerous and that no one called the police. Obviously, he'd been right to worry this morning about being arrested and defrocked.

Kate was certainly looking at him as if he was a criminal.

Which was probably the punishment he deserved for flirting with her—had he really been flirting?—without his collar on and without saying he was a minister.

He held the receiver to the side of his face and said, "Mrs. Ryan, you found me."

Chapter Three

Kate was surprised her lower jaw hadn't hit the floor. Her mouth had already been hanging open ridiculously at the idea that she might have been both flirting with and getting advice from a priest! And to have him confirm it like that—

She made a tiny sound of outrage, one he clearly heard, because he turned toward her, and for just a moment their eyes met, hers blazing, his contrite, and then he went back to his conversation.

That rat, she thought, because that was much, much easier than examining the guilt she felt, both for talking with a complete stranger about her feelings for Joe, when she hadn't found the courage to talk to Joe himself, and for kind of flirting with the priest.

Was it really flirting?

Honestly, she'd never been that good at either recognizing it or doing it, preferring a much more direct approach. So maybe that wasn't what they'd done. True, she had thought he was cute for a moment but, really, that was it. She'd spent maybe ten minutes with the man, in a public waiting room and on a public street. They'd done nothing but talk. So she really hadn't done anything horrible.

Except flirt with a priest, while she was engaged to someone else!

Kate groaned again.

Ben Taylor handed the phone back to Melanie and then turned to Charlotte and said, "I'm afraid I have to go. Can I call and reschedule?"

"Of course," Charlotte said.

And with that, he was gone.

The minute the door closed, Kate, Melanie and Charlotte all started talking at once. Charlotte's low, insistent voice cut through the other two, as she said, "What's going on?"

"He's a priest?" Kate asked.

"He must be. That woman kept telling me there had to be a man in a clerical collar in our offices, and I said there wasn't. Finally she said Ben Taylor, and I just about choked."

"Wait," Charlotte said again. "What's wrong?"

"He was trying to pick Kate up, right here in our reception area," Melanie said.

"Surely not," Charlotte said.

"He was. Tell her," Melanie said.

"I don't know what he was doing, but… He seemed so nice."

"But he's a priest. What's this world coming to, if you can't trust a priest?" Melanie said.

"He was trying to pick you up?" Charlotte asked. "Right here?"

"I think so," Kate said.

"He definitely was," Melanie announced.

She should know. She was much more of a flirt than Kate had ever been. Distressed and feeling even more guilty, she turned to Charlotte and said, "How do you know him?"

"I don't, really, but I'll find out all there is to know about him," Charlotte promised. "Don't worry."

But Kate did worry.

He'd thrown her completely off balance.

She prided herself on being a good judge of character, and she'd liked him right from the start. He had kind eyes with little crinkles in the corners and more at the corners of his mouth, which made her think he must smile a lot and generally be a pretty happy guy. He seemed a little too easygoing for her, but then most people were a lot more easygoing than Kate was. She didn't understand it, but she knew it wasn't always a bad thing.

He had a nice voice, strong and smooth and easy to listen to, and he was a very good listener. So few men were. So she'd talked, and he'd listened, and she'd told him everything she didn't want to even acknowledge about her and Joe, things she been avoiding for months.

"I have to go," Kate said, knowing if she stayed she'd really face an inquisition from Melanie and maybe from Charlotte, too.

"We'll be in touch about your first meeting with your little sister," Charlotte said.

She mumbled a thanks, picked up the satchel that doubled as both a purse and a briefcase, and fled.

It was a quick four blocks from Charlotte's office to Kate's own. She breezed in, asking her assistant Gretchen to try to get Joe on the line before she changed her mind. Ben Taylor might be a jerk, but he'd shamed her into taking action. Kate sat behind the closed door of her office with her palms sweating, trying to figure out what to say. All too soon, Ginny buzzed her and said Joe was on line two.

Kate picked it up and said, "Hi."

"Kate. Hi. Are you okay? You sound funny."

"I'm… I don't know what I am, Joe. You and I need to talk."

"Okay. Talk."

"Not now. Not like this. Where are you?" She thought he was still out of town, but couldn't say for sure. What did that say about their relationship?

"St. Louis," he said. "I was hoping to be home today, but it's not looking like I will. I'll have to see how things go, and then see what the airlines can do for me."

"Okay. Call me when you get in?"

"Sure. Kate? Did something happen?"

"No. Not really."

"You sound like something happened," he insisted.

And he sounded like he'd been expecting something to happen. What was that about?

"I just need to ask you some things," she said. "About us."

"Oh."

Oh? He said it as if it had a dozen different meanings, each fraught with possibilities.

What was going on? She'd been leading a perfectly sane life this morning. She had a business she ran well, a family she loved, a mother she was still mourning, true, but all in all, a good, sane, predictable life.

Was this punishment for showing up at Big Brothers/ Big Sisters under the guise of doing something nice for someone, when all she'd really wanted was to get in good with Charlotte Sims's husband?

She did feel guilty about that part.

But good work was good work, right? Were her motives really that important, when in the end she'd be doing a good thing? At least, she'd intended to do a good thing. She certainly hadn't gone there to flirt with a priest and question everything there was to her five-year relationship with Joe, who really was a very, very nice man. A sane man. A responsible one. A careful one. A smart one. A kind one. Everything she thought she'd ever wanted in a man.

"Katie, you're scaring me," Joe said.

"Sorry. I'm really sorry. I just… I have to go. Call me when you get into town, okay?"

Joe promised that he would.

Kate hung up the phone and wished with every fiber of her being that her mother was alive and well and that she could run to her and spill out all her problems to her.

She missed her so much. It had been horrible, watching her waste away like that. Kate had always thought she was so strong, that she could handle anything, but losing her mother had left her feeling as lost as a little six-year-old, like the little girl she'd helped to the car earlier.

She didn't know what was right or wrong anymore. She couldn't be certain about anything, even marrying Joe.

Tell me what to do, Mom. Couldn't you just tell me what to do?

Two hours later Ben was back, seated in front of Charlotte Sims, feeling like a naughty kid who'd been summoned to the principal's office.

"I am not a Catholic priest," he said. "I'm a minister at Grace Cathedral on Elm Street. Ministers in our church get married. No one cares. In fact, people think it makes us better at our jobs to have spouses and children, to better understand the kinds of emotions and challenges that come with marriage and parenthood."

"All right," Charlotte said. "So you were trying to pick up an engaged woman in my waiting room because…?"

"I didn't pick her up. I had a conversation with her. I thought she was attractive, and I thought just maybe I might leave with her phone number, that I might ask her to dinner or something. But that's it. And I didn't do any of those things because I found out she's engaged."

Maybe, he added. Was it *maybe?* Or was it *really and truly engaged?* He still wanted to know. No way he was asking Charlotte Sims about that. She'd probably slap his face, and rightly so.

"Melanie said you were flirting with Kate, and Melanie should know. She's one of the biggest flirts in the entire state."

"Well, then…I guess I was flirting. Guilty. Shoot me, please. Put me out of my misery."

"I can't. You owe me a favor."

Ben clamped his mouth shut, thinking he hadn't said a single, right thing all day.

"If," Charlotte added, "I decide I want you to have anything to do with my organization."

"I am not a bad guy!" He nearly exploded with it. "I just…I'm having a bad day, okay? I thought she was pretty. She was nice to that little girl, Allie, and I don't think I've spent a moment on anything that might be considered a personal life since I came here seven months ago. Obviously, I'm lousy at it. I am still single at thirty-two. I don't think I've had a serious relationship in the three years I was in divinity school or the two since I was ordained. Maybe I should have been a Catholic priest and given up on women all together!"

Charlotte stared at him. Slowly, he came to realize that the ends of her mouth were twitching, were fighting it seemed to curve upward into a smile.

"You think this is funny?"

She nodded, covering her mouth with her hand, giggles spilling out of her until her eyes filled with tears and she needed a hankie to wipe them away. Her shoulders shook. She was trying mightily and failing to keep from grinning.

"I am so sorry," she finally managed to say. "I just wanted to hear your side of it. I know all about you. I talked to Betty at the high school, and she told me Mildred Ryan is your secretary. I went to school with Mrs. Ryan's granddaughter, Peggy, so I put in a call to her. They assured me that you're a very nice man and a wonderful minister, even if you are a bit...socially challenged."

"Socially challenged?" he repeated.

Charlotte nodded, still fighting the giggles.

Okay, so they didn't think he was pond scum, just completely inept in the area of personal relationships.

You deserve it, Ben. Admit it. You do.

It was probably better if Kate went right on thinking he was a rat. Then she'd never speak to him again. He deserved that. That's why he hadn't tried to explain things to her before he took that phone call. He'd be better off if she stayed away from him, and he could only hope he hadn't done any permanent damage to her relationship with her fiancé, if the man still was her fiancé. And Ben wouldn't so much as look at another single woman for another seven months, at least. He didn't have time for one, anyway.

Charlotte finally managed to stop laughing. She dried her tears daintily with a delicate, embroidered handkerchief and then gave him a bright smile.

"Well. I guess we should get down to business. You owe me a favor, right?"

"Yes." And to think all he'd done yesterday morning was to follow a troubled, hideously dressed, pregnant teenager from his church and walk through a few open doors, thinking to do his job and help someone?

"How many people in your congregation on an average Sunday morning?" Charlotte asked.

"Maybe a hundred."

"Okay. I'm thinking ten percent would be good," she announced.

"Ten percent of…?"

"Your congregation, volunteering with my organization."

"Ten people? You want me to find you ten people?"

She nodded. "You're in the business of encouraging good works, right?"

Ben nodded.

"So, go encourage. Preferably people between the ages of twenty and thirty. And they have to have references and pass a background check."

"I doubt I have ten people in that age group in the entire congregation."

"I really don't care if they come from your congregation. I need ten more volunteers. Actually, I need more like fifty, and you look so wonderfully guilty about what happened earlier…."

"Okay, I'll find you ten."

"You know, you're getting off easy, Pastor."

If having to find her ten volunteers was the worst thing that came out of today, he was.

"And let me give you some advice," Charlotte said. "When you're striking a bargain, never agree to anything without knowing what it's going to cost you."

"I'll keep that in mind," he said. "You'll find someone for Shannon?"

"I'll get her the best person I can find," Charlotte promised.

"Good. Thank you." It was more than he deserved. "Now, what would you say are the chances of this little incident staying between you, me, Kate and your receptionist?"

"About a million to one against it," Charlotte said. "I'll be good, and I bet Kate will keep quiet, too, but Melanie… Well, one of the reasons she's so good at this job is that she knows just about everyone in town and all their secrets, which means she's always talking to everyone about everything. Sorry, Pastor Taylor."

He shook his head. "Not your fault."

It was his completely.

Maybe this was why Mrs. Ryan thought he should stay in the office and wait for people to come to him— because he was dangerous, loose out in the world. And he really should keep his clerical collar on at all times. It was just so unseemly, trying to meet women with the collar on, because they all jumped to the conclusion that he was Catholic. Not that he needed to be meeting women anyway. Look at the trouble it had gotten him into today.

He thanked Charlotte Sims for her help, apologized again for the mix-up, ignored the laughter that followed him as he left Melanie in the reception area, and went back to his office to be scolded by an eighty-year-old great-grandmother look-alike.

Charlotte Sims liked to think she had good instincts about people, and sometimes she got impulses to meddle, which got her into trouble.

Her instincts said that Pastor Ben and Kate Cassidy had protested too much that absolutely nothing had happened between them in her reception area, which meant that something had, maybe something special.

And Melanie's instincts told her that if Kate and her fiancé were ever going to get married, they'd have done it long ago. Charlotte remembered when she'd met Charlie. She'd been besotted, right from the first, and there wasn't anything in the world that could have kept them waiting for more than five years to be man and wife. Nothing.

There was careful. There was getting to know each another. There was the need to be sure, but five years was something else completely.

So…maybe it was up to her to do them all a favor.

That's how she thought of it.

A favor.

She had to find someone for Shannon, whom she'd met the day before, and Shannon's problems seemed much more serious than Allie's. Allie was a delight, and the distant cousin who'd taken her in seemed like a very good woman, though a bit frazzled, who'd provide a good home for Allie. And Charlotte could find a big sister for an adorable six-year-old blindfolded and with one hand tied behind her back.

So…maybe she didn't have to meddle with Kate and Pastor Ben.

Maybe she could just do the best she could for Shannon and things would fall into place.

She put in a call to the love of her life, her husband, Charlie. He was president of the local Board of Realtors, and at the group's annual dinner three nights ago, she'd managed to convince five of the people there to sign up as new volunteers with Big Brothers/Big Sisters.

Which meant that he had some connection to the only adult volunteers she had who had yet to be matched up with a little brother or sister. Two of them were men, which left three possibilities for Shannon Delaney.

Her husband came on the line.

"Hi, honey. I need your opinion about something. That secretary from your friend Tom's office? The one who's volunteering for me? I need someone who can handle a fifteen-year-old. A tough one. What do you think?"

"Sorry, darling. She's a nice lady, but I just don't think she's tough enough."

"Okay." Charlotte closed the folder in front of her and reached for another one. "What about the decorator? Gloria Sandling?"

"Well…she wouldn't be my first choice. Didn't Kate Cassidy sign up?"

Charlotte grinned. "Yes, she did."

"If you've got a tough case, Kate's your girl, honey. Smart, stubborn, responsible, knows her way around kids. She helped raise her two younger sisters after their father died, and she doesn't know the meaning of the world *quit*."

"Sounds perfect," Charlotte said. And she had not done this. Really, she hadn't. "It's just that she asked for a younger child. In fact, she met a cute six-year-old in our office today."

"Trust me, honey. Give Tom's secretary the six-year-old, and give your problem child to Kate."

"Okay, I will. Thanks, Charlie. I love you. You're so good to me. And so useful a man to have as a husband."

"I do my best, darlin'."

His contacts worked wonders for her when she needed volunteers or money, and he wasn't shy at all about exploiting those contacts for a good cause.

She told him she'd see him soon and then hung up, puzzling over exactly how to handle Kate. She had practically promised her the six-year-old, and she did feel guilty about that. But Shannon was in trouble, and it had nothing to do with Charlotte wanting to meddle in Kate and Ben's lives.

She was just doing what was best for Shannon. She'd pair Kate up with the girl, and if in the course of helping Shannon, she and Ben Taylor had reason to get together, well…Charlotte would leave that up to fate.

Kate got home that evening to find her middle sister, Kathie, who was also her roommate, on the phone in the kitchen, and by the look on Kathie's face, she had to be hearing all about Kate flirting with a priest!

The combination of guilt and curiosity in her eyes was all too clear.

"You know," Kathie looked absolutely pained as she broke into the conversation, "she just walked in the door."

"No," Kate mouthed. Whoever it was, she didn't want to talk to them.

"Oh. Okay," Kathie said into the phone. "I'll tell her."

Kate winced as she stepped out of her heels. Not even caring about neatness tonight, she left them by the coffee table along with her satchel and headed for the kitchen, loitering just outside the door, while Kathie stood in it, looking even more guilty as she managed to get rid of the person on the phone.

"Let me guess," Kate said, as her sister hung up. "Someone couldn't wait to tell you about the priest who was flirting with me?"

"Huh?" her sister said.

"That wasn't—?"

"You were flirting with a priest?"

Kate groaned aloud. "Who was that?"

"Joe."

"Even better," Kate muttered. She wondered if he'd heard about her and the priest yet. Honestly, that man had made her so mad. How dare he presume to give her advice on handling her relationship, when all the time he was just trying to get her phone number so he could ask her out?

"What's going on?" Kathie asked. "Joe said— Well, he thought something was wrong. That something had happened. Did something happen?"

"I don't know," Kate said, ridiculous as that was. It was her life. If anyone knew, it should be her.

"Why was a priest flirting with you?" Kathie asked.

"I don't know. Because he's a jerk?" But he hadn't seemed like a jerk. He'd seemed like a perfectly nice man. That I'm-no-good-with-women thing... She'd bought that completely.

"So, Joe heard about a priest who was flirting with you and—"

"I don't know." Kate was nearly in tears, and she never cried.

Her sister looked upset, too. Really upset. What was that about? Maybe just because Kate was so upset, and it took a lot to get her this way. Maybe Kathie thought something awful had happened.

Kate sniffled and swiped away tears.

"Did I do something?" her sister asked.

"No."

"Because, if I did… Joe seemed to think something was really wrong, and you're crying. You never cry. And…well, if it's me…I'd never want to do anything to hurt you. You know that, don't you?"

Kate was absolutely bewildered. "What are you talking about?"

"I don't know," her sister said.

It was like a disease, spreading through the kitchen. The I-don't-know-what's-wrong disease. It had been such an odd day.

"What did Joe say?" Kate asked.

Kathie hesitated, studying her sister, finally saying, "That he wasn't going to make it home today. Hopefully tomorrow. That he'd call you as soon as he knew for sure. But…he sounded like he thought you were going to break up with him. Are you going to break up with him?"

"I don't know," Kate said.

Her sister started to cry, too, then. Maybe everyone was having an awful day.

"I'm sorry," Kathie said. "So sorry."

"Me, too." She didn't even know for what, but she was sorry, and she gave her sister a hug.

"I miss Mom," Katie said.

"I do, too."

And they both stood there, completely miserable, crying for reasons Kate couldn't begin to understand.

Chapter Four

Shannon Delaney was back in church the next morning before school. Ben spotted her slipping into the sanctuary that morning soon after he arrived.

He'd already been lectured by Mrs. Ryan and promised to stay right where he belonged, safely in his office, that day. Truth was he was scared to go out into the streets, almost too scared to open his mouth around Shannon. It was no telling what kind of trouble he might cause.

Shannon walked up to the pew where she'd sat yesterday and sank into it, waiting for him, he thought. He walked over to her and found her staring, not sure what was going on at first, then realized he was wearing his white collar today. He might never take it off.

Still, she stared. He fidgeted, tugged at it and finally said, "Is it that hard to talk to me when I'm wearing this?"

"It's just weird," Shannon said.

He gave her wild, spiked, jet-black hair, pale face and black lipstick a slow going-over and said, "If you say so."

She glowered at him. "You seemed so nice yesterday."

"Not everyone thought so."

"Bad day, Pastor?"

"Definitely."

"Well, I didn't have a great day, either."

"Want to tell me about it?"

"No, I just... That thing you said? About God helping people who ask for it? Except, the help might not be exactly what you ask for or expect?"

Ben nodded.

"You think the help could come this fast? I mean like...yesterday?"

"Sure," he said, suppressing a grin.

She shook her head. "I mean, it seems like someone's trying to help. I don't know if it really will help, but it seems like someone is trying."

"Then let them," he said.

"That's it? Just...let them?"

"Don't make it harder than it has to be, Shannon."

"Why would anybody help me?"

"Why wouldn't they?" Ben asked.

"Because I'm not a very good person," she confessed.

"I don't think you're so bad."

"Still, it just seems weird that anybody would want to help me."

"You're thinking like a human being," Ben said. "You think people only help you if they like you or they think there's something in it for them. You're thinking you have to be good and deserve help to get it or maybe that you just have to be lucky or earn it somehow. God doesn't work like that. He just likes to help people."

"Sounds kind of silly to me," she said.

"Really? I thought it would sound pretty good to you, considering the situation you're in."

She frowned at him. "So...I'm supposed to...what?"

"Try to be open to the possibilities."

"Okay."

"Anything else?" he asked.

"Well...if God really did send someone to help me, I was thinking, I ought to thank Him, you know?"

"Yeah. He'd like that."

Maybe Ben hadn't messed up everything; as he'd feared.

Kate woke up that morning not sure what had hit her.

Her nice, sane life seemed to have tilted on its axis, and she wasn't sure where she'd gone so wrong, but she must have, because things seemed to be slipping out of place. She really liked having everything in its place.

To start with, she overslept, something she never did, because she'd hardly slept all night. So she was groggy and grumpy and rushing, which she hated. Kathie had already left by the time Kate walked into the kitchen, which was unusual. They almost always shared coffee and a bagel before leaving for work. This morning, when Kate finally got to the office, Gretchen was already there and already had a stack of messages for her, which she rattled off one by one.

"Brother, brother's fiancée, sister—"

"Which one?" Kate interrupted, as Gretchen peeled off little pick message slips and put them on Kate's desk.

"Kim."

"Nothing from Kathie?"

"No. She's the only member of your family who hasn't called." Gretchen gave Kate a puzzled look.

"Okay. Who else?"

"Melanie Mann, Melanie Mann, Melanie Mann. She says she's with Big Brothers/Big Sisters. Sounds urgent."

"It's not," Kate said. It was about her and the priest.

"She's calling every fifteen minutes," Gretchen said.

"Just keep taking messages, please? Did anyone call about work?"

"No."

Kate groaned. Just when she needed a crazy day at the office to keep her mind off everything else, it turned quiet. Perfect.

"Oh, wait," Gretchen said. "Someone from the Board of Realtors called, something about a committee for next year's home show?"

"I'm never going near the Board of Realtors again," Kate said.

"Why?"

Because that's what started all of this!

"Okay, I'm probably exaggerating a bit. Maybe. I just…" No way Kate was explaining. "Next time I open my mouth to volunteer for anything, stop me, okay?"

"Sure. Ready for coffee?"

"Please. I'll spring for espresso from the café, if you'll go get it."

"Deal," Gretchen said.

She was back before Kate even knew she was gone, delivering caffeine and saying, "Okay, I'll be at my desk. Who do you want to talk to this morning?"

"No one," Kate said.

"No one? Sisters? Brother?"

"No."

"Joe?"

"Especially not Joe."

Gretchen frowned. "Are you okay? Is something going on? Because I've had two phone calls myself from friends of mine who said... Well..."

"What?" Kate didn't want to know. Really, she didn't.

"That you broke up with Joe. Or that he broke up with you."

"Anything else?" Kate dared to ask, ready for something about the priest.

"No."

Kate closed her eyes and let out a breath. "We didn't break up. I just don't want to talk to him."

Which didn't make a whole lot of sense, now that she thought about it.

Gretchen waited, probably looking for more information. Kate offered none.

"Okay," Gretchen said again. "I'll just be out here, taking messages, all day. No one gets through. I can do that."

She probably thought Kate was nuts all of a sudden. Wait until the priest rumors started making the rounds. Then the phone would really ring off the hook.

"Ahh!" Kate groaned, not able to hold it in any longer...

The door popped back open. Gretchen stuck her head in. "What was that?"

"Nothing," Kate insisted. She must have been louder than she realized. Either that or Gretchen was listening at her door. "All I did was volunteer with Charlie's wife's organization!"

"Big Brothers/Big Sisters, right?" Gretchen said tentatively, hovering in the doorway, half in and half out.

"Yes. Charlotte brought it up in front of Charlie, and you know Charlie. He knows everyone. His firm is the biggest one in town. Just getting a little bit of his mortgage referral business would be great for us, and he loves it when people volunteer to help his wife's organization."

"So you volunteered? To get in good with Charlie?"

"Yes," Kate confessed. "I went yesterday, and there was the cutest little girl, Allie, with wild, kinky, curly hair and no front teeth. She wanted me to be her big sister, which I said I'd love to do. And I was thinking it was okay, even if I'd come for the wrong reasons. I mean, sometimes good things just happen, right?"

"Right," Gretchen said.

"But then... Well, then—"

"Is this the part where the priest started hitting on you?" Gretchen asked.

Kate groaned once more.

Kate hid quite skillfully all day. It wouldn't last, but by 4:15 p.m., she'd successfully avoided all contact with anyone but her clients, their attorneys, their real estate agents and the myriad of other people involved in getting people into a home of their own. The only nonwork item that got through was from Melanie, telling her that her little sister could meet her at 5:30 p.m., if that worked for Kate.

Chicken that Kate was, she had Gretchen call to confirm.

The meeting was set for Magnolia Falls Park, a long strip of land that ran along the river though town. Kate arrived promptly at 5:25, excited for the first time since the whole Big Brothers/Big Sisters debacle began.

She couldn't wait to see Allie again. Surely things would go smoothly from here on out, at least between her and her new little sister. With two real sisters of her own, Kate felt like she could hold her own with any little girl, especially one as outgoing and happy as Allie. All Charlotte asked was that Kate touch base with Allie once a week, hopefully get together for two hours or so, the activities of their own choice, from educational to pure fun.

Pure fun had never been Kate's forte, but maybe Allie could teach her.

Once the girl arrived.

Kate stood at the meeting spot—next to the ice cream stand in the midst of Magnolia Falls Park—at precisely five-thirty and fought the urge to pace.

The only young female she saw was…well, *frightening* was the first word that came to mind.

Nothing impish or cute about this girl.

She might be thirteen and she might be twenty. It was impossible to tell. She wore a little ribbed tank top that clung to her uncharacteristically pale skin. A disreputable-looking black leather jacket and oversize black cargo pants with a huge black belt and what looked like army boots.

So…she definitely wasn't a shoe person.

She'd probably done that really bad dye job on her hair herself—inky black, of course—and had pierced her ears too many times to count, plus her eyebrows. She'd painted her fingernails black and managed to find purplish-black lipstick somewhere.

She pursed those wicked-colored lips and took a slow, deep drag off her cigarette, staring belligerently back at Kate and arching a blackened brow as if to say, *What is your problem?*

Kate nearly laughed at that. This girl was the one with problems.

She dismissed Kate with another smirk and started to blow smoke rings into the air, much to the annoyance of the ice cream man, who was trying to wave it away with his hands.

"It's not Halloween yet, is it, Kate?" Bernie, the ice cream man, asked.

The girl looked bored, as she took another puff on the cigarette, her gaze remaining dismissively on Kate.

"Not for another few days, Bernie," Kate said.

"Can I get you something, Kate?"

Nerves getting the best of her, she said, "Sure, I'll have a fudge bar."

He dug it out of his cart and Katie took it, handing him a dollar bill and thanking him.

No one else had shown up. This was the only ice cream cart in the park. It was in the same place every day. Everyone in town knew where it was.

Waiting impatiently, Kate wondered how much of her own life story she should share with Allie. Kate's own father died at the hands of a convenience-store robber when she was only eight. And of course, her mother died of cancer six months ago, when Kate was twenty-seven. Life had not been easy for her, and yet she thought she and her siblings had turned out okay, her current situation with Joe and that odd thing with the priest notwithstanding. There wasn't a wild, rebellious, indignant or irresponsible bone in Kate Cassidy's body.

Which made her think of the girl beside her. If Katie had to guess, she'd say the girl was at least wild and rebellious, and she seemed to have a good head start on indignant, just looking at Katie, in her favorite black suit and her pretty black pumps. How could anyone object to a classic black suit?

She glanced at her watch. Five thirty-four.

She ate her fudge bar. Ghoul Girl, as Katie had come to think of her, finished her cigarette and threw what was left of it down onto the ground.

"Hey," Bernie warned her. "That's not where it goes, and believe me, you don't want to find out what the fine for littering in this park is."

That earned him a glare, too, but the girl picked up the cigarette butt and threw it into the trash. Katie finished her fudge bar and threw it away.

Five thirty-seven.

She had hoped to make the 6:15 advanced-cardio-burn class at the gym, but time would soon become an issue. Katie pulled out her cell phone and paged through the numbers programmed in the phone, for Charlotte Sims's number. Charlotte, cheery as always, answered.

"Hi. This is Kate Cassidy. I was supposed to meet my little sister seven minutes ago, but she's not here. I was wondering if she'd called to cancel?"

"Katie. Hi," Charlotte said. "She's not there? I hope nothing happened. I've got her cell phone number right here. Let me try her and see. Can you hang on?"

"Sure." Thank goodness for cell phones. She tried to never be without hers. Although, a six-year-old having a cell phone...? That sounded a bit odd.

Charlotte put Katie on hold, and, oddly enough, someone else's phone rang. Ghoul Girl's. Even her phone was all black.

"Yes," the girl said into the phone. "Yes, I'm here. I was even early."

Oh, no.

"Sure," the girl said. "I can hang on."

"Darling?" Charlotte came back on the line with Kate. "She says she's right there. I don't know how you two could be missing each other."

Kate gaped at the girl, looking back at Kate with what she imagined was equal parts horror and disgust. Turning to put her back to the girl, Katie whispered into the phone, "I thought I was getting Allie. Remember?" Impish. Pigtails.

"I know. I'm sorry. I thought Melanie called you. We really needed someone for Shannon. I don't think it's going to be easy to get through to her, and when I spoke to Charlie about it, he said you were the one for the job. In fact, he said you can handle anything," Charlotte said, sealing Katie's fate then and there.

She couldn't have Charlie Sims thinking she couldn't handle one rebellious, frighteningly dressed, nicotine-addicted teenage girl.

"Oh," Kate heard herself say. "Okay. Whatever you need."

"Great. Her name is Shannon Donnelly. Don't let the look fool you. She's only fifteen and very, very intelligent."

Intelligent? No way, Katie thought, glancing at Shannon, who looked bored once again and was reaching for another cigarette.

"Call me later and let me know how everything goes," Charlotte said.

"Sure." Kate closed the phone and faced Miss Shannon Donnelly.

Shannon lit another cigarette, took a big puff and said, "Hey, sis."

Kate nearly choked. Surely this was her punishment for coming into this program for all the wrong motives and maybe for flirting with the priest and not facing up to her problems with Joe.

"What's the matter?" Ghoul Girl asked. "Scared?"

"Of you? Amused is more like it."

It wasn't a promising start, considering she was supposed to help this girl, but what could she do? Politeness wouldn't get her anywhere, Kate thought, and neither would kindness right away. She couldn't afford to let the girl think she was intimidated, either.

Time for some tough love.

Or…tough affection, maybe.

Tough help.

"You really do look like you dressed up for Halloween today," Kate said, testing her theory.

"And you look like an uptight old woman," the girl returned.

Okay. The girl respected toughness and bluntness. They could communicate on that level and work toward something more civil at a later date.

"Guess we won't be swapping fashion tips," Kate said.

"Guess not," the girl said, then hitched her chin up a notch and flung back, "So, you're just doing this to impress the director's old man?"

Oh, great.

The girl grinned. "I heard enough that I guessed that's what you might be doing. I mean, you don't seem like the do-gooder type."

"That's what got me started," Kate admitted. "Who twisted your arm to get you here? Because I can't imagine you coming here willingly, either."

The girl's composure slipped for just a moment, and she looked half human. *Okay.* They were getting somewhere. Kate wondered who had enough influence over the girl to make her do anything—and why that person hadn't forced her to do something about that awful hair.

"What if I didn't?" The girl shrugged.

"So, we've both got our reasons for being here, and neither one of us can back out. So…we might as well make the best of it? Getting together a few times should be enough to keep everybody happy, right?"

"Yeah," the girl agreed. "That'll work."

If anyone overheard the deal Kate just made, they'd think she was a really lousy person and still trying to impress Charlie, which she was.

But now that she'd met the girl…

She obviously needed help, and she looked like a real challenge.

Kate loved a challenge.

Besides, she liked fixing people. She happened to think she was great at it, although her siblings were starting to complain, something about her advice sounding more like meddling, that her need to have things in perfect order was starting to bug them. Kate was trying to cut back on her advice, but it was a tough habit to break. Maybe she could make this girl her project, instead.

"Why don't we start over? I'm Kate Cassidy." She held out her hand, which the girl pointedly ignored. Were they supposed to smack their hands together or something?

"Shannon Donnelly."

"Want to sit down?" Kate invited.

She got that I-couldn't-care-less shrug again, but the girl sat on the bench.

Kate sat beside her. "So, anything going on that I could help you with?"

"I don't think so." Shannon laughed again. "Anything I can do for you, Kate?"

"I doubt it." Kate sat there, racking her brain for something else to say. "I was pretty good in school, in case you need any help there."

"Like I'd care about school? Please." Shannon rolled her eyes dramatically. "How old are you, anyway?"

"Twenty-seven."

"And everything's startin' to go, huh? The body? The face?"

"Hey?" Kate frowned. "I thought we were going to make this as painless as possible for each other? Could I get a little cooperation, please?"

"Look, I don't need anything from you," Shannon said, looking like a little girl for maybe a split second, if that was possible under her disguise. "I don't need anybody. So, what do we have to do? Look at each other once a week or something? Is that it?"

"I think that's it."

"So…" Shannon got up. "Here? Next week? Same time? That work for you?"

"That's fine." Kate opened her purse and took out a business card. "Take this. Just in case something comes up. Like…you can't make it or something. Don't leave me standing here, okay?"

"Yeah. Sure."

"Shannon?" The girl finally stopped still for a moment and looked at Kate, who felt a strong urge to do something more. She was just a child, just fifteen, and she seemed achingly alone in this world. "The offer's good for anything. You never know. Believe it or not, I'm good at solving problems."

"Yeah? Me, too. I give out advice all the time. Like… what to wear for Halloween and stuff. You got a costume, Kate?" The smirk was back.

"Not yet."

"I could loan you something of mine. And…hey, this would be funny. You could loan me something of yours, too, and I could go as a first-class, uptight b—"

"Hey! We were going to be nice, remember?"

"Yeah. See you next week."

Chapter Five

Shannon left the park with her stomach in knots. She'd done what Ms. Williams said she had to do. She'd met with the woman, and Shannon would see her next week and the week after that, if that's what it took. Nobody ever said Shannon and Miss Uptight had to get along, just that they had to see each other.

Fine.

Shannon did a lot to simply get along in this world. Seeing a way-too-serious woman in a horrible black suit was far from the worst thing she'd done.

Her stomach rumbled as she walked, maybe from hunger, maybe from the fussiness it had displayed of late, and she wondered whether it was safe to eat or if the food would just come right back up. She held a hand over her belly, refusing to think about what was inside, just knowing that she wouldn't be able to hide it much longer, and she had no idea what she'd do then.

If someone was going to send help her way, they'd better do it soon.

Yesterday she'd thought maybe help was arriving, but not anymore. Ms. Williams had gotten mad at her for missing school and threatened to report her to the office. That would have meant a three-day suspension, which would have meant not seeing Paul at all, because school was the only place she saw him now.

Shannon couldn't handle three days without him. Then Ms. Williams said she'd forget the absences if Shannon would enroll in the Big Brothers/Big Sisters program. Shannon was about to refuse, but then she remembered what Ben had said—about sometimes not recognizing help when it came your way. She'd thought maybe this wouldn't be so bad. Maybe it would actually help.

Should have known better, she thought.

She didn't expect much from anybody. Not the boy who'd done this to her or the woman she'd just met in the park. Not from her father or the priest or God.

Just when she was feeling good and sorry for herself, it started to rain.

"Oh, great," she muttered, hunkering down as best she could inside the leather jacket. It wasn't the warmest thing, but at least the rain ran right off it.

She had more than a mile to walk before she got home. Not that she wanted to be there or to even see her father. He hated her hair, her clothes, her piercings, her makeup, the things she said, the way she said them, the expressions on her face. Basically, everything about her. If they passed each other in the house, she looked the other way and tried to keep her mouth shut. He worked nights mostly, and if she was lucky, slept during the day and went out in the evenings. Sometimes he left money for food, and sometimes he didn't. Either way, she got by. She wasn't bad at picking someone's pocket or getting what she really needed from the grocery store, and she didn't even feel that bad about it anymore.

A girl had to eat, after all.

She stepped in a puddle, the water soaking through the hole in the bottom of her boots—cold, wetness soaking through her socks all the way down to her toes.

Great.

As she rounded the last corner to the rundown duplex where she and her father lived, she saw a car she didn't recognize in the driveway.

Immediately she thought there was some kind of trouble.

She'd have turned around and gone the other way if the front door hadn't opened, revealing her father and a very well-dressed woman.

"That's her?" The woman grimaced at the sight of Shannon.

"Yeah, that's her. Shannon, get your butt in here right now."

Shannon couldn't imagine what she'd done to upset the woman. She was all made up and put together, looking like she was afraid of getting dirty or something, and the car looked brand-new, like it probably cost more every month than the place where Shannon and her father lived.

"Now!" her father said.

Shannon stood just inside the doorway, not going any farther.

"This woman says you know her son," her father said, "that you're trying to cause trouble for them."

Shannon gaped at the woman. Paul didn't look or act

like a rich kid. Not that they'd talked that much or anything. But still she was surprised.

"You are the one, aren't you?" Mrs. Bradshaw said. "The one who's after my son?"

After him?

No, she was just having his baby.

It might be stupid, but it hadn't been a calculated move on her part, and it had taken both of them to get her this way.

"My son is going to college, like every other member of his family has. We have plans for his future, and no one is going to get in the way of that. Do you understand?"

Shannon nodded slowly.

"If you're looking for money, you can take your chances with my husband and his lawyers, but I doubt you'll get far. If you really are pregnant—" she glanced pointedly at Shannon's mid-section, now protected by Shannon's own arms "—the first thing we'll insist on is a DNA test, so you might want to rethink your plan or whether you actually know who the father of this baby is."

"Is it true?" Her father jumped in. "You were stupid enough to let yourself get pregnant?"

Shannon started shaking. She didn't want anything from Paul or his family, not like this, but her father was standing right in front of her, too. She had no idea what he might do, once she admitted she was pregnant.

Her chin came up, and she tried as best she could to look like someone who didn't care about anything. "I guess I'll just have to rethink my plan."

Mrs. Bradshaw smiled, thinking she'd scared Shannon into admitting a lie. "I thought you'd see it my way. I trust we won't hear anything else from you?"

"No, you won't."

"Good." She nodded dismissively at Shannon's father and then left.

Shannon's father's face had turned a blotchy red. He'd probably been drinking again. She wondered how much?

"So?" he growled. "What's the story? You pregnant?"

"Yes," she admitted.

He swore long and loud. "Is that snotty old witch's boy the father?"

"Does it matter?" Shannon asked.

"Do you even know who the father is?"

Shannon glared at him, refusing to allow anything he said to hurt her.

"Just like your mother," he said. "I'd be surprised if she knew for sure you were my daughter."

"You'd probably have denied it, if I hadn't come with a social security check every month, right?" It wasn't much, but it was all they had sometimes.

Her father swore once again and for a minute, she thought he was going to hit her. A part of her wanted to goad him into it.

"Never mind," he said. "Just get out."

"What?"

"You heard me. Get out. I'm done with you. I'm not having you and your brat in this house. I'd never get any peace, and I'm not paying for a baby."

"But...where am I supposed to go?"

He laughed. "Shoulda thought of that before you got yourself knocked up."

He practically shoved her out the door, with nothing but her school backpack, shoved her back into the dark and the cold and the rain.

Of all the situations Shannon had imagined when he found out, this wasn't one of them. She thought he'd yell, maybe knock her around a little bit, but mostly she'd thought he really wouldn't care, that he'd ignore her the way he'd always done, and she'd be in this all by herself.

She never thought she'd be out on the streets.

She was so shocked at first, she just stood there, not knowing what to do. The rain fell down upon her, mixing with her tears.

She looked up the street and down. She didn't have anyplace to go. There had been friends, pretty good kids, before her grandmother died, but their parents hadn't appreciated Shannon's turn to the dark side—her stupid hair, the piercings and the tough-girl mouth she'd adopted to go along with the look. She was no longer welcome in a lot of places, where at one time she'd have gone for help.

She started to walk, then saw the church where she'd actually believed for a moment that someone—maybe even God—was going to help her. Shannon laughed until she cried some more, and then she stormed up to the front of the church, yanked on the door and got nowhere. It was locked up tight.

"Ahhh!" she screamed, frustration building even higher.

As she turned to go, she nearly tripped and fell over a crumpled piece of sidewalk. Fury swelled up inside of her until she picked up the concrete and hurled it in the direction of the church. It made a thoroughly satisfying thump when it hit the door. She liked it so much, she picked it up and threw it again and again and again, until it crumbled up to almost nothing.

"You're really helping me now, aren't you?" she screamed at the door.

She found something else to throw. It shattered against the door, just as it opened, narrowly missing the head that popped out.

"Hey?" a man's voice called out. "Watch it!"

She recognized that voice. Shannon thought about running, but she was too mad. Some of the blame for this was his, and she intended to tell him about it.

"Shannon?" He stepped outside and stared at her through the darkness. "What are you doing?"

"What am I doing? What are you doing? Telling people you'll help them? That God will? What a crock!"

"What happened?" he asked. "What's wrong?"

"Everything's wrong." Her voice broke, and she started sobbing. "I thought you were going to help! You and your church and your God. I really believed that for all of a day. I thought things were going to get better!"

"Okay, you need to calm down and come inside and tell me what's wrong. I'll help. I promise."

"No one's going to help me," she said.

"I will. Just give me a chance—"

"I'm all out of chances. There's no point in even trying. Everyone leaves. Everyone dies. Everyone disappoints you. Everything hurts—"

"Sometimes," he said softly. "Sometimes it does. But it won't always be that way. I promise."

She laughed bitterly. "You don't know that. You can't possibly know."

"Just come inside," he said. "Get out of the rain. Get warm. I'll get you something to eat. I'll take you anywhere you want to go. Please—"

"There's nowhere to go," she cried.

And then she turned and ran.

* * *

"So, how did it go?" Charlotte Sims asked when Kate picked up her cell phone and answered the call as she drove home.

"It was interesting," Kate said.

Charlotte laughed. "Don't let the look put you off. Until about eight months ago, Shannon was a fairly normal teenager, if there is such a thing. It's all in her file. I'll have someone drop it by for you tomorrow. Kate, you should know, I have about a hundred kids on the waiting list for big brothers or sisters right now. I moved Shannon to the top because two people made an urgent request on her behalf. They're very worried about her."

So, where were they? Kate pulled into her driveway and shut off the car, not knowing what to say.

"Look, it was just a first meeting," Charlotte said.

"I know." Kate got out of the car and walked in through the garage door.

"You probably did more good than you realize this afternoon."

"I certainly hope so," Kate said, walking into her kitchen and finding her fiancé sipping a cup of coffee with her sister.

She stopped abruptly, had actually forgotten that she'd told him they had to talk about something important and that he was supposed to be back in town today. Just what she needed. A conversation with someone else who she suspected really didn't want to talk to her.

"Charlotte, I have to go," Kate said.

They said goodbye. Kate snapped her phone closed and put it down on the counter, along with her keys and her satchel. She was about to say something when her mother's dog, Romeo, a gorgeous Australian shepherd, and the new love of Romeo's life, a white poodle-like thing named Petunia, rushed to greet her.

She bent down to fuss over Romeo, because he expected it, and then to pick up Petunia and hug her for a minute. They both gave her big smiles, and Petunia wanted to kiss her, but Kate fended her off. Her brother took care of Romeo, now that their mother was gone, and Petunia belonged to his fiancée. If anyone tried to separate them for too long, Romeo cried like a baby.

"Hi." Kate gave her sister a panicked look. "We're dog-sitting?"

Kathie nodded. "Jax is pulling a double shift, and Gwen's visiting her mother. And…I'm going to my room."

Petunia started to trot after her, but stopped when Romeo didn't follow. She looked unhappy not to have his full attention, which she was used to. Romeo stayed in the kitchen, as if he knew something was up. Joe looked as though he did, too.

Kate couldn't put off facing him any longer. She offered him her cheek. He kissed her briefly and impersonally, as if she'd seen him a few hours ago and not nearly a week ago. His coat was thrown over a nearby chair and his bag was on the floor beside it. "You came straight from the airport?"

"Yes." He stood awkwardly, looking as if he was a stranger instead of a man she'd known for more than five years and been engaged to for a year and a half.

Kate made a cup of hot tea to give herself something to do, thinking, as the silence descended between them, that she and Joe really didn't have much to say to each other. Surely at one time she'd loved him. He'd seemed perfect for her. As serious and sensible and hardworking as she was—a calm, steady, dependable man who seemed to want exactly the same things she did in life.

Where had that gone?

And it should hurt, to think that it was all gone, shouldn't it? Kate tried to look inside of herself and find the hurt, because she'd been accused of not really letting herself feel anything, of shielding herself as best she could from most everything, and the idea that she was like that had certainly hurt.

But losing Joe, here and now? Did that hurt?

It certainly wasn't pleasant. But she wasn't devastated, either, and suddenly the thing she needed to do seemed perfectly clear.

She put a hand on Romeo's furry head, to steady herself, and said, "Joe, you don't want to marry me anymore, do you?"

He looked startled.

And, she would swear, incredibly relieved.

He tried to cover it quickly, but she'd already seen it.

So, she'd been right.

That hurt, too. She felt as if she'd failed in some way—that there'd been love between them and they'd lost it. Maybe Kate had lost it. Kate, who had trouble allowing herself to feel anything.

"Do you still want to marry me?" Joe asked quietly.

Fine. She wasn't sure if he was trying to spare her feelings or was just too honorable to go back on the promise he'd made. So she'd say it for him.

"I don't think I do," she said, twisting the ring he'd given her off her finger and holding it out to him. Romeo pressed closer to her side and made a crying sound, the one Kate wouldn't allow herself to make.

"No," Joe said, gallant to the end. "Keep it."

"Really, no. Besides, I have one of my mother's rings that won't fit any other finger but this one, and I haven't been able to wear it. Now I can," she said stupidly. As if she'd break an engagement so she could wear the ring her father had once given her mother. "Please, just take it."

Joe did, pocketing it and then looking up at her once more. "I'm sorry."

"Me, too," she said, willing herself to leave it like that, but she just couldn't. "Did I do something?"

"No. It's not you. It's me. I mean…"

Obviously, he'd just remembered that he hadn't broken it off, she had, and looked horrified at what he'd just given away.

"You just don't love me anymore?" she asked, fighting the urge to sink down to the floor and put her arms around the dog, whom she knew still loved her. Did love between a man and woman just fade away? It seemed as though people would be able to point to an event or a time and say, *There. That's when we lost it. We had it here, and then we got there, and it was just gone.*

"I care about you," he said. "I always will."

"But you don't love me?" Voices came to her, her own inside her head, filling in with the words he would not say. That she was cold, unfeeling. That she expected too much from people. That she tried too hard to be perfect herself, and who wanted to live with someone like that?

Of course, Joe wasn't exactly the life of the party, and he would never wear his emotions on his sleeve. They were alike in so many things.

She needed to understand what went wrong. Understanding meant you'd learned something, and learning meant that maybe next time, you'd do things differently. You'd be smarter and better prepared and maybe successful, if wise decisions and preparation and careful thinking worked in love. The problem was, she didn't think they did.

"I don't think what we feel for each other is strong enough to get us through the things couples face in a marriage," Joe said. "Do you?"

"No." But she still didn't understand why. A silly thought flitted through her head. A ridiculous thought. *Not Joe.* "You didn't meet someone else, did you?"

And he looked even more guilty than before.

Kate gaped at him.

Romeo growled.

Joe hung his head. "Nothing happened, Kate. I swear."

Romeo growled once again, outraged it seemed.

"What does that mean?" Kate asked, trying to shush the dog with a hand on his head. "That you met someone—"

"Yes," he whispered. "I didn't go looking for this, Kate. Please believe me when I say that. I wouldn't do that to you."

"Okay." Oddly enough, she believed that. Joe looked as shocked about the whole thing as she felt. "So, this woman…"

"She was just there. I…In front of me. And…nothing's happened between us, I swear, but—"

"You wish it had," she finished for him.

"Yes."

"More than you want to be married to me?"

"I can't be married to you and feel this way about another woman. I can't be engaged to you and feel this way about anyone else. It's not fair, and I'm sorry I let this go on as long as I did. I kept thinking it would just go away. That maybe I had cold feet or something, and I'd come to my senses. I swear, Kate, sometimes I think I've lost my mind."

Wow. Joe, crazy in love? It was hard to imagine. He'd certainly never felt that way about her. In fact, she'd been relieved, mostly, that theirs had never been a crazy-in-love kind of thing.

That would have scared her, no doubt. The fact that it had never been crazy was probably the only reason she'd been able to let herself love him. Or think she was in love with him.

Nothing too messy or emotional for Kate.

She wondered if her mother had known, if this was why she'd insisted they not rush their wedding so she could see them married before she died.

Kate would have liked her mother to have seen her married. She'd have liked her mother to be here right now, so Kate could pour out her troubles, and her mother could hold her and say all the right things, and make Kate feel better.

But there was no mother.

And now, there was no fiancé.

"I'm sorry, Kate." Joe leaned down and kissed her one more time. "I wish there was something I could do to make this easier for you."

She shrugged. "If you figure out how this works? The crazy-in-love part? Let me know."

That was Kate.

More worried about analyzing than feeling.

No wondered Joe didn't love her.

Chapter Six

Ben found Betty's number in the church directory. She hadn't seen Shannon, but promised to call if she showed up. Betty offered to call a few friends Shannon might turn to for help. Ben checked out a few teenage hangouts, a local coffeehouse, a secluded parking lot near the falls, an old-fashioned drive-in restaurant, finding nothing. From the restaurant parking lot, he called Betty back. She had no ideas left, except Charlotte Sims's home phone number.

Ben called from the car. "Look, I know it's a long shot," he said, "but have you by any chance matched Shannon up with a big sister yet?"

"Yes," Charlotte said.

"Have they met?"

"This afternoon," Charlotte said. "What's wrong?"

"I need to find Shannon. She was throwing rocks at the front door of my church tonight, screaming at me and God, saying there was no one who could help her and that she had nowhere to go, right before she ran off into the rain. I have to find her. I want to check with her big sister, just in case Shannon turned to her."

"Oh, my. I paired her up with Kate Cassidy."

Kate?

"Why?" he asked.

"Because you said she really needed help, and someone I trust who knows Kate told me she could handle anything. I did what was best for the girl."

Okay.

Ben hadn't even tried to explain himself to Kate. She'd looked so shocked and so angry, and he'd thought he deserved having her think the worst of him and that they'd probably never see each other again, anyway.

"She's a reasonable woman, Pastor. She'll listen to you," Charlotte said. "Besides, you have a mutual goal. You both want to help Shannon."

"I don't suppose you could tell me how to get in touch with Kate?" he asked, and just like that, he had her address and her phone number, the thing he'd wanted so badly when he'd first met her.

Now he was afraid to call.

Shannon wandered around for what felt like forever, especially in the cold rain, but was probably only about an hour.

Ms. Williams would take her in, but everybody knew about the trouble the assistant principal had made for her last year when she'd gotten caught taking in another one of her students who'd run away from home. Over the years, she'd probably fed and housed more teenagers than a runaway shelter, but the parents of the last kid hadn't know where he was for a few days, and they'd made a stink about it. When the school found out, they'd threatened to fire her if she did it again, and there was no way Shannon was going to risk getting her fired. She was the only adult who was even halfway nice to Shannon anymore.

Shannon went through her pockets, one by one, coming up with nothing but a black lipstick, eighteen cents and a business card with Kate Cassidy's phone number.

She frowned at the number, rain dripping stubbornly upon it. She could try to find Paul, just to make his mother even madder, but they lived on the other side of town. It was late. She was cold and tired and maybe even hungry.

Odd that she'd end up with nothing but a business card from an uptight-looking woman she'd just met for the first time that day. Shannon could just imagine Kate Cassidy's face if she called. In a perverse way, she liked the idea of calling Kate's bluff. After all, she'd said if Shannon needed anything, all she had to do was call.

Shannon's stomach rumbled in protest. If anything, the rain was falling harder and faster. There was a café on the corner that looked like it was open. She walked inside, wondering if she'd ever be immune to the stares and whispers that followed her everywhere she went when she was in her Halloween costume, as Kate had put it.

She walked up to the counter and said to the woman who'd just finished ringing up an order, "Do you have a phone book I could use for a minute?"

No attitude at all in her voice now. She couldn't summon an ounce.

The kind-looking woman in a bright-blue apron and

awful glasses pulled one out from under the counter and put it down between them.

"Thanks," Shannon said, hoping to find Kate's address. There. K. Cassidy at 41 Sugarcane Lane. It wasn't even that far from here.

"You need the phone now?" the woman asked.

"No, thanks. I just got turned around, trying to find my friend's house."

"Nasty night to be out," the woman said. "You okay?"

Those few kind words were almost enough to bring Shannon to tears. She was more of a mess than she thought.

"Yeah," she insisted. "I'm fine."

"Want some hot chocolate before you go?" the woman asked. "On the house?"

She was already pouring it into a cup, steam rising from it. Shaky all of a sudden and so grateful she couldn't even stand up anymore, Shannon sank onto a stool. The woman placed the cup in her cold, wet hands, the warmth already seeping through it and inside of her. Next thing she knew, the woman, whose name tag read Rose, had brought her a towel to dry off with and offered her a ride.

"Really. I'm okay. I have a place to go," Shannon insisted.

Besides, it would be harder for Kate to turn her down if she was standing there, dripping wet and cold, on Kate's doorstep.

As Shannon finished her hot chocolate, Rose whispered to her that if she ever needed a meal, she could get one here, to just find Rose and she'd take care of it.

Shannon wiped away tears as she slipped out the door. Sometimes people were truly kind. It always surprised her when that happened, and it seemed when she was angriest or feeling the most hopeless, someone like Rose would come along.

Or maybe Kate Cassidy.

Or maybe the priest at the church.

She hurried down the block, then went east for two blocks and then south for one, and there she was, at the door of a neat, modest, pale-brick home. From the looks of things, Kate had brought out a ruler to trim the bushes that lined the front of the house to the exact same height and width, and planted the flowers in regimented rows. There probably wasn't a single thing out of place in the entire house.

Why had Shannon ever thought she'd even get in the front door?

She ended up walking around the block about six times. Finally she worked up enough nerve to ring the bell.

Footsteps came from inside, and then Kate's voice saying, "Coming."

The door swung open in a *whish,* and there stood Kate, her hair still up, that boxy, black suit still on, a big, furry dog by her side and a silly, little white one by the big one's side.

"Surprise," Shannon said.

Kate looked at her blankly. The dogs sniffed, then waited to see if she'd pet them. She hadn't expected Kate to have dogs, especially not ones like this. Kate would have something with a pedigree that didn't dare shed or make a mess, one that hardly made a sound. These two looked much too normal to be hers.

"Yeah, I know," Shannon said. "You didn't invite me over. But you said if I needed anything… And I know this definitely isn't what you had in mind, but do you think I could crash here? Just for one night? Because I really don't have anyplace to go."

When the doorbell rang, Kate had thought for a moment it was Joe, coming back to say he didn't mean what he'd said before, that he still wanted to marry her. That they were so well-suited and got along so well.

But it certainly wasn't Joe.

Kate wouldn't have been more surprised if the Tooth Fairy had shown up at her door.

Which made her think of Halloween costumes.

It really wasn't Halloween and yet Shannon still looked dressed for the night, although she'd kind of wilted and gotten smudged in the rain. And she was shivering.

"Come on in," Kate said, shoving back the thought that once she actually let the girl in, it would be much harder to get her back out.

Immediately she felt guilty for the thought.

If her mother were alive, she'd have let Kate have it, even for thinking of not letting the girl in out of the rain. She'd have been ashamed of Kate. Kate was ashamed, too. Maybe she really had become an uptight witch. Maybe that's why Joe didn't love her. Maybe she didn't deserve to be loved.

Shannon stepped inside, to the delight of the dogs, who grinned up at her, panting and swishing their tails back and forth. Petunia did a little dance, wanting to be picked up. Kate closed the door, thinking from the look on Shannon's face that she might want to pick up the dog but wouldn't do it for fear of ruining her tough-girl image.

She probably wouldn't believe it if Kate admitted it, but she'd spent a good, solid fifteen minutes sitting on the floor with Romeo cuddled against her side and Petunia in her lap, Kate aching with loneliness and the dogs trying to comfort her.

"You've got to be freezing," Kate said, glancing over the girl. "Do you have any clothes in that backpack? Or is it just school stuff?"

"School stuff," Shannon said. "Sorry about this. Really. If I could just stay the night, I could find someplace else tomorrow. Promise."

Kate grabbed an afghan from across the back of the sofa and held it out to the girl. "Jacket off first. And, tell me. Did you run away from home?"

"No. I got kicked out." Shannon shrugged out of the jacket.

"Just drop it on the tile. I'll hang it up later. Why did you get kicked out of your house?"

"Ahhh, you know." Shannon shrugged and let Kate wrap the afghan around her. "I mean, you've met me. You can't be all that surprised, right?"

This close to the girl, she seemed so short and thin. Like there was nothing to her but leather and attitude and makeup. Fifteen seemed much younger than it had only hours earlier.

"What did you do?" Kate asked.

The girl moved away from her, leaning against the door and one, pale, shaking hand holding the afghan around her. "Made my old man mad. No big deal. He's always about to stroke out about something."

"So, he has no idea where you are?"

"Lady, he doesn't care, as long as I'm not bugging him."

"Really?" Kate asked.

"Is that so hard for you to understand? Did you grow up in one of those weird families where you had a mother and a father, and they got along and actually stayed together, and you have siblings that you actually still speak to or something? Maybe have dinner with on national holidays?"

"No, my father was shot and killed when I was eight," Kate said. That usually bought her some ground with anyone who tried to say she'd had it made growing up. "But I do still speak to my siblings, and we do have dinner together. It doesn't even take a holiday."

Shannon frowned at that. "Look, I know you're not supposed to be my mom or anything. I got the lecture about what not to expect from you, and you and I made that deal anyway about just making this look like it's working out—"

"It's okay. You can stay," Kate said.

"Huh?" The girl looked vaguely hopeful and very, very surprised.

"I could see where you were going with all that and decided I could do without the speech. Plus, you're shivering. Why don't you take a hot shower and I'll find you some pajamas. Nothing nearly as fashionable as the stuff dripping onto my floor, of course, but warm, I promise."

The girl blinked back up at her and, for once, said nothing. Romeo woofed happily, seeming to know she was staying. He loved company.

"Could we make a deal about the makeup, too?" Kate asked. "Maybe you could take it off? Just while you're here? You might frighten my sister."

"Your sister's here?"

Kate nodded. "We live together. Sweet, isn't it?"

"Oh, yeah. She scares easily?"

"Yes."

"How old is she, because if you've got a little kid around—"

"Twenty-four."

Shannon frowned, as if she couldn't be sure whether Kate was teasing her or serious, as if there might really be something wrong with her sister Kathie.

Kate's mouth twitched as she fought a smile. "Don't worry. She's normal as can be, and she won't bother you.

"My brother has his own place, and so does my other sister, Kim."

"Wait, your parents named you Kate, Kathie and Kim?"

"Yeah, I know. It's a miracle anyone can keep us straight. My father's family had a thing about alliteration and daughter's names. Some kind of tradition I've never understood." Kate sighed. "Try not to make a joke about it. I've heard them all. I was about to make some dinner. Want some?"

Shannon said no, but her stomach chose that moment to growl loudly.

"I'll take that as a yes. One more thing. No smoking in my house," Kate said.

"Okay."

"Come on. I'll show you the bathroom and get you a fresh set of towels."

Kate turned over the supplies, then went into the kitchen and stood there, gazing around the room as if she wasn't sure she recognized the place.

Actually, it looked like her place, nice sturdy furnishings, pretty, pale colors on the walls, stark-white cabinets with a black granite countertop she'd had installed last year, because it would raise the value of the house, of course, and not a thing sitting on the countertops. There wasn't an object out of place or an ounce of clutter, except maybe in her sister's room.

This was her house. It just wasn't her life.

She'd lost a fiancé in this room, less than an hour ago, and she'd somehow gained a sullen, gaunt-looking, sad-eyed teenager who could hardly stand Kate but obviously had no place to go.

What kind of a trade was that?

As she stood there, something her mother always said popped into Kate's head—that we might not get what we want in life, but we usually got what we needed.

Kate couldn't see how she might need a teenage girl more than Joe. But then, her mother's faith had always been much stronger than Kate's. All Kate was certain of was that life was hard, really hard. It didn't make much sense, and it kept surprising her, often in unpleasant ways.

Kate heard the shower come on and remembered she had a guest to feed. Looking through her cabinets, she saw that canned soup was her best bet, and maybe some bread. She had frozen dough that turned into warm rolls fairly quickly and smelled fabulous, even if they did come out of a freezer bag. Her mother always said the world never looked quite so bad over a good meal.

While she started the soup and the bread, she grabbed the phone and called her brother, Jax, who was a policeman.

"Hi, it's me. I have a quick question," she said. "You don't have any reports of missing teenagers in town, do you?"

"Why? Did you find one?"

"No." Shannon had found her, Kate reasoned. "I just want to know if anyone's reported a teenage girl missing today?"

"Not today," her brother said. "And I'm on duty, so I'd know."

Which meant that whoever Shannon had left behind wasn't looking for her. Did that mean it was okay to keep her?

"Want to tell me what's going on?" Kate's brother asked.

"Not really. But will you tell me if anyone does file a report on a missing girl?"

Her brother made an irritated sound that meant he didn't understand why his sisters didn't just tell him everything he wanted to know, right away, without any argument. "Want to give me a name?"

"Shannon. She's fifteen."

"Does that mean if I needed to find her, you could be of help?"

"Maybe," Kate said. If the girl stayed.

"Katie, what are you doing?"

"I don't know. She said her father kicked her out, and that she needed a place to stay, just for the night."

"Her parents could be going crazy trying to find her, and just not have called the cops yet."

"I know."

"Want me to call?"

"No. I can't have her thinking I went to the police—"

"I don't have to tell them I'm a cop. I'll just call and ask for her, and see what her father says. Or I'll get Pete Simmons to. He sounds like he's about sixteen."

"Okay. That would be good. But no cop stuff. Her name is Shannon Delaney. I don't even have a phone number for her yet."

"It's all right. I'll find her."

Kate thanked him and hung up the phone. Having a brother for a cop came in handy at times. He'd been a rock to her, her sisters and their mother growing up, but now that he was getting married soon, she felt he was slipping away from them. She was happy for him, but uneasy about all the changes taking place. Her baby sister had just graduated from college, and her mother had died. Kathie, with her, was still blessedly normal and Kate was—*unsettled* wasn't the right word. It wasn't big enough or messy enough to describe how she was feeling.

Lost? That worked.

Sad? Bigger than that.

Alone? Very, very alone. That was the worst word of all, and it fit perfectly.

Before she died, Kate's mother had said Kate kept her feelings locked up too tight and that one day, they were going to come pouring out.

And then what?

She'd drown, she feared. If they all came pouring out at once, she'd drown.

Kate's sister Kathie walked into the kitchen a few minutes later, frowning as she saw her sister. "I thought you were in the shower. If you're here, who's there?"

"Company. My little sister. Shannon. She just showed up, cold and dripping wet, saying she didn't have anywhere else to go. She's spending the night."

"Oh. Okay. You do that kind of thing with the Big Sisters program?"

"I don't think we're supposed to." At least not without the parent's permission.

Kathie did a double take. "You mean…you're breaking a rule?"

She said it as if Kate might have just announced she was flying to the moon.

"Yes," Kate said defensively, as she stirred the soup.

Kathie put her hand on Kate's forehead. "Do you feel all right?"

"Not really, but what am I supposed to do?" Kate pushed her sister's hand away. "It's late. It's raining. It's cold. And I'm not going to call Social Services at this hour. She probably just had a little spat with her dad. I mean, come on… I told you what she was like. If you were her mother, and she looked like that, can you imagine the fights you'd get into?"

"Yes, but still…"

"I'll probably just take her home in the morning and they'll patch things up and everything will be fine."

"And if not?"

The phone rang, saving her from having to answer. Kate grabbed it. It was her brother. "What did you find out?"

"Her father said he doesn't know where she is and doesn't care, that he doesn't expect her back anytime soon. And then—are you sitting down?"

"No. Should I be?"

"Definitely," her brother said.

Kate sat on a stool. "Okay. Tell me."

"After he told Pete he didn't expect her back anytime soon—"

"Yes?"

"He asked if Pete was the father of the baby she's carrying."

"She's fifteen," Kate said, as if that meant the other wasn't possible.

"Yeah. It happens. More often than you'd think and to girls even younger than she is. What are you going to do with her now?"

"I have no idea." She thanked him, hung up the

phone and told her sister. "Well, I guess we're keeping her for a while, because she's pregnant."

"Wow. You know, there are agencies that take care of kids at times like this."

"I know, but she came to me, and I...kept thinking of mom. She would never have turned Shannon away."

"Of course not."

Kate opened up the oven to look inside to check on the rolls. They were done. She pulled them out and turned the oven off, then blurted out. "Am I such a bad person that you're shocked that I'd try to help this girl?"

"No. Not bad. Never bad."

"Just judgmental and too hung up on rules to ever ignore them in order to help a cold, wet, homeless, pregnant teenager?"

"I didn't say that."

No. Her sister didn't have to say it.

"I have to help her," Kate said.

"That's fine. Really." Kathie looked around, puzzled. "I forgot—where's Joe?"

Oh, hell. Joe. Kate felt weary just thinking of him. "He left."

Her sister looked puzzled by that, either because of the tone Kate used or the brevity of her answer. Kathie looked as though she had a lot of questions about Joe, questions Kate didn't feel up to answering at the moment. She had to think, to figure out what she was going to say to people. How did one announce an unengagement?

"Okay," Kathie said, when no explanation was forthcoming.

"Anything else going on?" Kate hid her face behind the refrigerator door, looking for butter. How long could she sell the idea of looking for butter, when the refrigerator was as organized as the rest of the house?

"Well, Kim called this afternoon. She found an apartment. A big two-bedroom place on Sixth Street, part of an old house that's been broken into apartments."

"Great," Kate said. Kim was their youngest sister, just twenty-one years old, and had just graduated from college after the summer session. She'd taken a spot in a house with four other people, but they were driving her crazy and she wanted out. "She'll need a roommate. Money's going to be tight with her just starting out, and teaching school… I mean, I'm happy she's teaching, if that's what she wants. But she's never going to make a lot of money."

"I know." Kathie looked uneasy.

Kate gave up on hiding in the refrigerator and started buttering the rolls. "Surely we know someone who's looking for a roommate."

"Well…actually, I was thinking I might move in with her," Kathie said. "I mean…you and Joe…I'm sure you'll be setting a date soon, and whether you move in here or into his place, you won't be in the market for a roommate anymore, and… Well, I just thought it would make sense. Don't you think?"

Oh. Kate should have seen that one coming. It would make sense, if she and Joe were going to get married. But they weren't… Of course, her sisters didn't know that yet, and if Kate told them now, they wouldn't get the apartment. It would mess up all their plans.

Kate loved plans. Plans made everything easier, she believed. She especially loved it when her sisters made plans, because she worried they didn't do it often enough. The last thing she wanted to do was mess with a good plan. Plus, if anyone should be living alone, it was her. She was the oldest. She was supposed to help take care of her sisters, and she made more money than any of them.

Great plan.

So why did she feel as if she was being abandoned?

Which reminded her of Shannon.

"Oh," Kate said. "That would be great. Then if Shannon needed to stay for a while, she could have your room."

She said it with a forced smile she hoped her sister wouldn't notice. She'd wait until they signed the lease on the apartment and then tell them about her and Joe. It would be too late for them to back out on the apartment then. Her failed engagement couldn't be allowed to mess up her sisters' lives. All she needed was for Joe to play along for a day or so, and he felt guilty enough to do just about anything right now.

"It makes perfect sense," Kate said.

Her sister looked so relieved she knew it had been the right thing to do. And yet, there was something… Kate couldn't say what, but something that had her thinking there was more going on with Kathie than Kathie had said, too. Was Kate a lousy roommate? Was she so hard to live with? So…picky and set in her ways? Was that part of why Joe didn't want to live with her, either?

"You're sure?" Kathie asked tentatively.

"Absolutely." Fake-smile time again. How long could she hold it without her face cracking under the strain?

Something weird was going on here.

Kathie would tell her if something was wrong, wouldn't she?

Unless she worried that Kate wouldn't understand or sympathize? Unless, maybe, she worried Kate would give her a little lecture and talk to her about being careful and making plans. Not that Kate's plans were working out at the moment.

Like when her mother died, this thing with Joe had Kate thinking the worst thoughts. Such as…maybe planning didn't matter at all. That it was useless against life's little tragedies, like losing people she loved. What good was a plan if it didn't keep her safe from blows like that? She wondered if she was moving into some odd cycle of complete disarray. She'd always thought strings of personal disasters that happened to other people were completely avoidable with nothing but a good plan, but now she wasn't so certain.

It was as if she could feel all sense of control slipping though her fingers as she sat there buttering rolls and thought about not having Joe, about not having her sister here with her and having a walking ad for Halloween costumes in her shower and about a priest flirting with her, all things she wouldn't have thought possible not two days ago.

She had no plan anymore, she realized.

It was terrifying.

Chapter Seven

Ben spent a good fifteen minutes contemplating his own cowardice toward his secretary, Kate Cassidy and possibly even Shannon Delaney, and another fifteen thinking of his general uselessness, until he was thoroughly sick of himself and ashamed. It took that to get him to Kate's house.

Defrockment didn't sound so bad at the moment, as he wondered what in the world he'd say to Kate.

If he hadn't balked at kidnapping, Shannon would be safe and warm and well fed, and her baby would be, too. But, no. He'd let the church cleaning lady and his secretary scare him into refusing to break the law, and look what happened? He lost track of a pregnant fifteen-year-old, maybe for good.

He got out of his car, walked morosely up the front walk and knocked on Kate Cassidy's front door. It was still raining miserably, and he was cold and hungry and feeling sorry for himself, too. Perfect time to meet a woman who he thought had great legs—a woman who now despised him.

She opened the door a fraction of an inch, safety chain engaged and frowned up at him, as if she was having a nightmare that included visions of him. A dog stuck his nose out and sniffed.

"What are you doing here?" Kate said in an outraged whisper.

"Looking for Shannon Delaney. Is she here?"

Kate frowned even harder. "What do you have to do with Shannon Delaney?"

"I got her into Big Brothers/Big Sisters," he admitted.

Which sent the door slamming in his face.

He stood there and wished he could swear without feeling guilty, but then the door swung open, minus the chain, and Kate, looking all rumpled and cute in flannel pajamas with what looked like drunken reindeer on them, said, "You got this girl into the program and assigned to me?"

"No," he insisted.

Her dogs, a big one and a silly, little one, gave him the once-over but decided to reserve judgment for the moment. He didn't even try to befriend them.

"Do you have no shame at all?" Kate asked.

"I do. A great deal, actually, about a number of things—"

"I'm not surprised at that," she announced.

"Oh, stop it! I'm not Catholic. I'm an Episcopalian priest. There's a difference. I'm not breaking any vows by...by—"

"By what?"

"You know what," he said. "Although, I am sorry for

that. I shouldn't have done it. I should stay out of your engagement. I don't know what came over me. I haven't been on a date in about two years. Can we put it down to that?"

"You're allowed to date?"

"And get married and have children and all that stuff, not that I'm likely to ever manage the marriage part, and if I did the kid part without the marriage, I would be in trouble. I'm just bad at the whole man-woman thing, okay? And I'm not so great at being a priest, but I'm not a jerk, either."

He was almost shouting by the time he was done, and the big dog was growling, the little one hiding behind the sofa. Water was dripping off his face, because he hadn't brought his umbrella, and he was cold and very, very grumpy, not that he had any right to take it out on her. Just because she had nice legs and was kind to tiny, motherless girls who'd lost their hair ribbons, and he'd gotten ideas about her and him that would never come to anything.

"Sorry," he said. "About everything. Is Shannon here?"

"Yes," Kate admitted.

"Is she okay?" he added quickly.

And then, maybe because Kate saw that he really was worried about the girl, she eased up on him a bit.

"She's obviously upset, but she got a hot shower, dry clothes and some dinner. She must have been exhausted, because she's sleeping."

"Thank God," he said. Then, because she obviously wasn't going to ask him in, he said, "Could I come in? Just for a minute?"

Kate made a face at him, but stepped back and opened the door.

So, it was that painful just to let him into her house? *Great.*

She left him standing in the entranceway, dripping on the tile floor. There would be nothing resembling a warm welcome.

"Did she tell you what happened?" Ben asked.

"Her father kicked her out."

"Son of a—" He clamped his mouth shut, barely. "Sorry. He found out she's pregnant?"

Kate nodded.

Well, that explained that. Shannon had come to him for help, and then, not a day later, her whole life had gotten worse.

"How do you even know her?" Kate asked.

"She showed up at my church looking for help."

"So…you got her into Big Brothers/Big Sisters."

"Something like that." He wasn't admitting to the stalking part. "She came back tonight throwing rocks at the front door and yelling at me. But she didn't stick around long enough to tell me what was wrong, and I got worried."

"So, you took off searching through town until you found her?"

"Yes," he admitted. "I finally called Charlotte, who told me she'd matched Shannon up with you—"

"Yeah, about that…"

"—which I had nothing to do with."

"Oh, right," Kate said.

It sounded like he could be the last man on earth, and she wouldn't believe a word he said. "I didn't," he yelled.

The dog growled again and took a menacing step toward him.

"Romeo, stop it," Kate said.

"You have a dog named Romeo?"

"No, my mother had a dog named Romeo. My brother takes care of him now. I'm just dog-sitting, and the little white one is his fiancée's dog, Petunia. She wouldn't hurt a flea, and normally Romeo wouldn't, either. But just so you know, he used to be a police dog. If I asked him to, he'd tear you apart."

Romeo growled, to prove it.

"I'm not here to hurt anybody," Ben said. "I just wanted in out of the rain."

He glanced pointedly at the floor, which he was dripping on, he was so wet.

"Oh, all right." Kate stalked off into the hallway, coming back with a towel, which she threw at him.

Romeo tried to snatch it out of the air, obviously thinking this was a game, but Ben got to it first. "Sorry to be such an imposition," he said to both of them.

"What do you know about this girl?"

"Next to nothing," he said, as he started to towel off. "I just met her two days ago. One of her teachers said she lived with her grandmother and was a pretty happy, normal kid, then lost the grandmother and moved in with the mother, who she'd hardly ever seen till then. Things were…not great, but okay. She lost her mother six months ago and ended up with her father. That's when things got bad."

"And the baby's father?"

"No idea," Ben admitted. "But I don't think she has even seen a doctor the whole time she's been pregnant. That's the first thing we have to take care of."

"We? What do you mean, we?"

"I'm not going to just forget about her," he insisted.

"She was throwing rocks at you earlier."

"She's a teenager. You have to expect a little drama," he reasoned.

"I have never thrown rocks at anyone in my life, and neither have my sisters."

"Ever been fifteen, pregnant and homeless?" he shot back.

"No, but that's no excuse. Throwing rocks doesn't solve anything."

"Maybe she's not as problem-solving oriented as you are."

Kate wanted to throw something else at him, but she really wasn't a violent person. The towel was bad enough. She took it from him, explained to the dog that he could not have it, then didn't know what to do or say. What a horrible day.

"She's terrified, Kate. Haven't you ever been terrified?"

The day her father died came to mind.

The day her mother's cancer was first diagnosed.

The day they found out it had come back.

The day she died.

Losing Joe and having no idea what had gone wrong.

Those days came to mind.

"Sorry," the utterly annoying man standing in front of her said ever so softly.

She realized too late there were tears in her eyes, falling unheeded down her cheeks and that, worst of all, he'd seen them. He took a step toward her, to do what, she couldn't imagine, but she put up a hand to hold him off. "I'm fine."

"No, you're not."

"I am. I'm fine!" Prickly as could be and a liar to boot, it seemed.

He took a breath and let it out slowly. She watched, not meaning to, but not looking away, as his shoulders slowly rose and fell with that breath. He had nice shoulders. Broad ones that were good for hanging on to when life was just rotten.

How long had it been since she'd hung on to anyone and cried? Or since the idea had sounded so good to her?

When her mother died? Had she hung on to Joe and cried?

She couldn't remember.

She was sure he'd offered and said all the right things, but taking him up on it would have meant admitting how horrible and lost she felt, and that wasn't something Kate let herself do very often. Even with Joe.

God, what was wrong with her?

"Bad day?" Ben Taylor asked, a wealth of understanding in his tone.

She remembered again how easy it had been to talk to him the day before, the way he seemed to really listen and let her come to her own conclusions. She'd like to blame him for what had happened with her and Joe, but it wasn't his fault.

"I'd offer to listen to your problems, but I figure you'd throw something at me," he said. "Something tougher than a towel."

"Oh, stop. I don't throw things. Not usually."

"I just bring out the best in you?"

He grinned then.

He was kind of cute.

In a priestly sort of way?

"You're really not…I mean…this is okay?" she tried.

"What's okay?"

"You being in my kitchen at this hour with me…" Dammit, she was in her drunken reindeer pajamas! She'd forgotten all about that. Honestly, when the doorbell rang, she was sure it was going to be Joe, telling her he'd been out of his mind earlier and that of course there was no other woman. That he loved her and absolutely had to marry her, right away. Panic had her wanting to go back to the way things had always been, the way she'd expected her life to be.

But it hadn't been Joe, and then she'd been so startled and so mad, she'd forgotten she was standing here in her flannel pjs.

"Nice jammies," Ben Taylor said.

She shot him a look that had sent lesser men cowering, but he stood firm, grinning. "A present from my sister two Christmases ago."

"Celebrating early?" he asked, because it was early October.

"I was cold, and these are the warmest pajamas I own."

"Like I said…nice. I didn't know reindeer got that happy."

"I think they've been drinking," she admitted.

"Didn't know they drank—"

"I'm sorry. It's late. I've had a rotten day, and I have Ghoul Girl in the bedroom I use as an office, and tonight I found out she's pregnant."

"Right. Sorry," he said again. "What are you going to do with her?"

"I don't know."

Three little words that were practically foreign to her before a year or so ago. What hope did she have of doing the right thing, if she didn't know what that was?

"She needs to go to the doctor for a checkup, at least. If I find someone who'll see her, will you take her?"

"Yes," she agreed. If the girl stayed around that long.

"Thank you. Sorry you had such a lousy day."

And then she nearly started to cry again.

"Kate—"

He took a step toward her, shoulders beckoning. It would feel so good, wouldn't it? To be in any big, broad-shouldered man's arms while she cried her eyes out? She backed up for every step he took, and he finally stopped coming toward her, threw his arms up in surrender to show he was no threat and then said with every bit of sweet understanding and acceptance he'd shown her earlier, "Is there anything I can do?"

"No."

There was nothing anyone could do. She'd just have to come to terms with all of it. How could she have been so wrong for so long about her and Joe?

"Okay," Ben said. "I'm going to start calling doctor friends. I'll find someone who'll see Shannon, even without insurance, and then...I'll call you, okay?"

Kate nodded.

"And I'll behave, and I know you'll behave, and we can help Shannon together. I won't ask about your love life or try to give you advice. I won't do anything to make you uncomfortable or to give your fiancé reason to worry. Deal?"

Kate planned to keep her mouth shut and nod. That was it. Instead, words forced themselves out, escaping her. "You don't have to worry about the fiancé. He's fallen for another woman."

There.

It was out.

She'd told someone, thinking it might feel better to stop holding it in.

Ben Taylor stood there, taking it all in. "You mean...yesterday, when we were talking...you just hadn't told anyone yet? You were hiding it?"

"No, I didn't know then. He just told me. A few hours ago."

"Oh, I'm so sorry."

Her bottom lip started to tremble, as if she was about to make some really pitiful, crying face and sob. She held most of it back, with effort.

"It's all right," she insisted.

"Sure it is," he said, not calling her on her little lie for once.

"I didn't really love him. Not the way I should have. I thought I did for a long time, but I didn't. Better to know it now than figure it out later." Like another five years from now.

"Yeah, but it still hurts."

"It does." She puzzled over that. "Doing the right thing shouldn't be so painful. It should be easy, shouldn't it?"

He shook his head understandingly. "I never thought about it like that, but yeah, it should be."

"I usually don't have any trouble figuring out the right thing to do."

"You want to go fight for the man? See if you can get him back?"

"No." The thought never occurred to her. "Not that. I meant…staying with him the way I have, all this time. It seemed right. I thought he was perfect for me."

"We all make mistakes, Kate," he said.

"Yeah." He'd said that yesterday, hadn't he?

"Sometimes it is painful to do the right thing. But it gets better. I firmly believe that. Keeping on with the wrong thing…that's what hurts in the long run."

"Promise it's true?" she asked, hating sounding like a little girl looking for reassurance.

"Yeah, I can promise. I have extensive experience in doing the wrong thing."

"Doing it yourself or helping other people who do it?"

"Both," he claimed.

She hoped so, because she was counting on everything to get easier from this point on. Otherwise she didn't know what she'd do.

Ben walked into his office the next morning whistling.

Mrs. Ryan was immediately suspicious.

"What have you done now?" she asked.

"Nothing," he insisted.

And he hadn't. He'd been a perfect gentleman, not improper at all with Kate last night, if he did say so himself. Other than the fact that they'd had the conversation late at night with her wearing drunken reindeer pajamas, there was nothing he could think of that would have worried Mrs. Ryan at all.

"I know you've done something," she said. "And I'll figure it out."

He tried to suppress a grin, but couldn't.

She really worried when he looked happy. It was unseemly, she thought. Priests should be a solemn lot.

"It's a beautiful day outside," he claimed. "Did you notice, coming in? The sky was still tinged with pink, and the sun was just coming up. Great day."

"Have you been drinking the communion wine? Because we had a priest here thirty-five years ago who did that. He looked just like you do this morning."

"No, I have not broken into the communion wine. I'm just happy." Granted, he wasn't usually this happy, but it didn't make him a lush.

Mrs. Ryan scowled at him, the way a teacher might look at a boy who'd just cut off a girl's pigtails. "You're not planning on going anywhere today, are you?"

"As a matter of fact, I am." He was going to the doctor with Kate and Shannon, as soon as he talked someone into seeing the girl. "Don't we know somebody who knows somebody who's an OB/GYN?"

"The undertaker, Frank Russell, the one people here hardly ever use because his prices are so high? You remember. He buried old Mrs. Parker not long after you got here, and you had to do the funeral, even though you hardly knew her, and you couldn't keep her daughters straight."

"Oh, yeah." Not his finest hour. They were triplets, and they all looked alike. The harder he'd tried to keep them straight, the more flustered he'd become.

"Frank Russell's son's a doctor."

"Great. Would you get Frank on the phone for me, please?"

"Frank Russell's the tightest man in the world. He's not going to do you a favor, and his son won't, either."

"Sure he will."

If it was one thing Ben had confidence in, it was his ability to get people to do things. Guilt was a wonderful thing, and he had no problem using it to help people who really needed help.

He had Shannon a doctor's appointment twenty minutes later.

Kate woke up with a plan.

She loved it when she had a plan.

All that business about plans not working and not protecting people from little disasters along the way…she just hadn't been herself yesterday. There must have been some cosmic disturbance. Solar flares or something. Hadn't she read those things made everything go wacko? Mostly electronics, but probably little things like people's sensible plans, too.

She was over it.

Back to the plan.

She had three big items on her list:

Do something with Shannon. Not sure what, but something.

Get her sisters to sign the lease on their new apartment ASAP, this morning preferably.

Convince Joe not to blab about their broken engagement yet, which should be a piece of cake, considering how guilty he felt about falling for someone else.

She was leaving something out, she knew—how she was going to handle Ben Taylor, and he definitely needed handling... Handling?

Kate blushed at her choice of words. She wasn't handling the man. She'd never touched him. She wasn't going to start now. She was going to make it clear to him that they were both merely interested in helping Shannon, and that was it.

No handling. No comforting. No freelance counseling sessions. No friendly advice. Nothing between them at all.

There. Four measly things she needed to accomplish today. She could do four things in her sleep. She often worked with a daily list of a dozen items or more. Come to think of it, she'd stopped making her daily lists months ago. Sometime right after her mother died, and look what had happened? No wonder her life was a mess.

Kate grabbed a pad of paper and a pen from the kitchen countertop and dutifully made out her list.

1. Sisters—lease.
2. Joe—quiet.
3. Shannon—doctor. That was it. First step, doctor.
4. Purely professional relationship only with B.T.

She thought about adding No Crying, but decided she didn't need to.

Done.

Great list.

She hummed as she picked up the phone to her sister Kim, bracing herself to put on a happy face, so that no one would have any idea of the night she'd had.

"Kim, hi. Sorry it's so early, but Kathie told me you found a fabulous apartment! I'm so happy for you. Listen, Kathie had the best idea last night."

"Huh?" her sister, the original sleepyhead said. "Have you had like five cups of coffee already?"

"No, only one." Kate would never have five cups of anything of a questionable nature healthwise. Granted, she loved coffee, but she got one cup at home before going into the office, one cup when she arrived, and if it was a bad day, one cup right after lunch. Never five, and never altogether in the morning.

"You just sound unusually perky," Kim complained.

"Sorry." She knew that annoyed people, especially early in the morning, and tried not to do it too often. "I just have a lot on my list today, and I wanted to make sure I got to look over the lease before you sign it. It's a huge financial obligation, and you should never sign something like that without having someone look it over."

"Okay."

Kate plowed ahead. Steamrolling her sister was so easy when Kim was sleepy. "I was thinking you and I and Kathie could meet at the apartment to look around and I could check the lease right there. If it's okay, you can sign it then."

"Wait. I don't have a roommate. I can't afford it on my own."

"Sure you do. Kathie. She'll explain the whole thing to you when you talk. Set up a time for us all to meet and then give me a call, okay?"

"Okay."

Still groggy. That was good. Kate just hoped her sister remembered having this conversation. She'd have her assistant call, just in case. One more thing for her list.

Kate said goodbye, then cheerfully put a check mark beside that item on her list. The checkmark meant she'd set that item into motion. When it was accomplished, she'd cross it off completely.

There was nothing like looking at a daily list and seeing everything crossed off.

Joe was next. She got his answering machine, wondered if he was ducking her calls, the coward. She left a quick message that might have sounded more like an order, but she didn't care.

"It's me. Don't tell anyone we broke up yet. I need to think about...how I'm going to do it. Give me twenty-four hours, and I'll get back to you." It was the least he could do after falling in love with someone else.

A big line went through that item on her list.

Ben Taylor called next. "Sorry it's so early," he said.

"It's not early."

"Oh. One of those people, are you?"

"What kind of people?"

"Let me guess. You're feeling better this morning? More like your old self?"

He said it as if that was a bad thing. "Of course."

"Okay. Shannon surfaced yet?"

"No, and I have to leave for work. I have a busy day."

"Time for a visit to the doctor at eleven?"

Kate mentally reviewed her schedule for the day. "Sure. Have you said anything to Shannon about this doctor's appointment?"

"No."

"So you don't know if she's willing to go?"

"No."

"Okay. I'm going to work," Kate said. "I'll leave her a note telling her to help herself to breakfast and that you're coming over at ten. You can get her there, right?

"You don't think I can?"

"I'm just saying…she's not the most agreeable person I've ever met."

"I can get her there," Ben claimed.

"Okay. I'll meet you there."

She said goodbye to Kathie, who'd overslept and was getting dressed, and the dogs, whom her brother would be picking up soon, and left.

Melanie Mann was at her desk right before lunch, when Beth Drayton, who was in her home room every year in high school, called from Dr. Russell's office. Dr. Russell delivered babies, and Beth was one of his clerks.

"You won't believe who I saw sitting in our waiting room together," Beth said.

"Who?"

"Kate Cassidy, and a guy who wasn't Joe! What did the priest look like yesterday?"

Melanie gasped. She'd have sworn they'd just met, right there in her office, but you never knew about people. You really never knew.

"Tall," Melanie said. "Kind of skinny, dark hair, dark eyes. Kind of cute, in a Clark Kentish sort of way. A little awkward. Kind of...brainy-looking."

Beth gasped. "That's him! I swear, that's him!"

"Kate's pregnant?" Melanie asked.

"Practically everybody in this office is pregnant."

Wow.

You really never knew about people, Melanie decided.

Chapter Eight

Kate was running late.

Because the doctor had been running late. Obviously a situation stemming from poor planning. And after they'd sat waiting for forty-five minutes, he'd gotten called to the hospital to a delivery and cancelled Shannon's appointment altogether!

Which meant the next day they got to do the whole thing again.

Kate could just see it: She and Ben sitting next to each other, Ben grinning because he just did that, even when he and Kate were snipping at each other, Kate checking her watch and her to-do list, plus taking calls on her cell phone; Shannon across the room in full Ghoul-Girl mode, no doubt giving all the young mothers-to-be nightmares about what would become of their babies.

She'd sulked and not said a word to Kate or Ben the

whole time they were in the office, although Kate might have seen a hint of fear in the girl's dark eyes. She supposed it would be hard to face indisputable proof of the life growing inside of her.

But that was a task for the next day. Now, Kate was rushing to the address Kim had given her. The landlord was waiting. The lease was waiting. Joe was waiting, just as she'd asked. If the apartment was even halfway acceptable, her sisters weren't leaving without signing the lease.

She arrived out of breath and looking…well, un-Kate-like, she supposed, because her sisters were staring at her, as was a little old lady with stark, white hair.

"Sorry I'm late," Kate said. They all kept staring. "What?"

"You're late," Kim said. "And you're never late."

"I know." Was it like a law? Everybody else got to be late, but not her? She wasn't a machine, after all.

"This is Mrs. Warren," Kim said, still looking oddly at her sister. "Mrs. Warren, this is my oldest sister, Kate."

"Hello, dear," Mrs. Warren said. "You're the one in real estate?"

"A mortgage broker," Kate said, relieved the apartment actually looked nice. She'd have felt guilty if she'd pushed her sisters into a place that wasn't nice, just to make Kate's life easier. "Great place. Lots of windows and light, nice big rooms."

"Come see the bedrooms," Kim said, dragging her off down the hallway and into both rooms and bathrooms.

Her sisters liked it. Kate saw no reason to disapprove. She read the lease twice, satisfied, looked at her sisters and felt a twinge about this time in her life coming to an end. They'd always lived together, if they weren't off at college. Kate knew it was unusual for a woman of her age to live with her sisters, but they'd all been unusually close since their father died and throughout their mother's illness.

But they weren't going to be together anymore.

"What's wrong?" Kim asked. "You looked so sad for a minute."

"I just...well, I'm going to miss you two," she said softly.

At which they both looked like they might cry, too.

"We don't have to go through with this," Kathie said.

"Unless the three of us and Joe are all going to live together," Kim said, laughing. "I don't think he'd like that."

To which Kate said nothing.

Finally, she pulled out a pen and handed Kim the lease. "It's a great place. You two have the money for the deposits?"

"Yes," they chorused.

"Not just for the apartment, the utility deposits, too?"

"Yes," they said.

Of course they would. She'd given both of them their financial educations, and they were well equipped young women, ready to take good care of themselves and their money, to make good decisions, and this was one.

"Then sign it," she said. "It's a great place. It's perfect for the two of you."

With great flourish, they both signed, then grinned and hugged each other.

There. One item to cross off her list.

Kate was late again, getting back to the office, and Gretchen seemed to be watching her closely, an odd look on her face.

Just because Kate was a few minutes late?

Her sisters had kept talking about plans for their apartment, and then she still hadn't had lunch, so she'd grabbed a sandwich to eat at her desk.

Kate sat down, reaching for her turkey on wheat. Gretchen hovered in the doorway, looking uncertain.

"Go ahead," Kate said. "Let me hear all the messages. You talk. I'll eat."

Gretchen started through the stack of little, yellow message slips one by one, moving unusually slowly. What in the world? She got to a hitch in a loan-closing scheduled. Kate mumbled an answer through a bite of her sandwich.

"Sorry," she said. "I'm starving."

Which only had Gretchen staring even more oddly.

Oh, geez.

What could have happened?

Had Joe blabbed to someone already?

Was the news already out?

Finally, Gretchen got to the last message. "A man named Ben called?"

"Yes."

"He said, 'Dr. Russell's office, tomorrow, eight-thirty.'"

Kate mentally flipped through her schedule for tomorrow, scribbling a note to herself to put into her Palm Pilot later, when both her hands were free.

"Okay, that works."

Gretchen just stood there. "Dr. Russell delivers babies."

"Yes, he does."

"Well…I just wondered…I mean, I thought you would have told me, but… Are you and Joe having a baby?"

Kate choked on a bit of wheat bread, had to cough twice before she got it to go down and could breathe again. "No!"

"Are you and this other man…Ben?"

"Of course not!"

"Because my cousin Ellen, who works at the bank, heard from someone, who heard from Melanie Mann, that you had an appointment at Dr. Russell's office this morning, and that the man with you wasn't Joe!"

Kate squeezed her eyes shut and made a face, probably that awful, I-have-to-scream-but-I'm-trying-to-hold-back face she so hated to make, because it was so unattractive and spoke of a complete lack of control.

"I am not pregnant!" she said.

"Are you seeing someone else? Other than Joe?"

"If I was, I wouldn't be dating him at the obstetrician's office!" Didn't people think these things through at all? It was no place for a date!

"No, I guess not. But—"

"And if I was pregnant, and I didn't want anybody to know, I'd go to a doctor in another town. Maybe another state!" That would probably be what it took to keep the whole thing a secret.

"This is about that man you met the other day, isn't it? The priest?"

"He's not a priest. He's a…well, he is, but he's not. He's not Catholic. He can get married and have kids and all that stuff without breaking any of his vows. Not that he's doing anything like that with me," Kate said.

"Okay." Gretchen frowned. "You just don't seem like yourself. Every since you met him—"

"Ever since I met him, my life has started falling apart!" Kate practically yelled. And it would feel really good to have someone to blame for that. She picked him. Ben Taylor. Freelance do-gooder and causer of all kinds of havoc. He'd told her the night before he was really good at making the wrong decisions. She was starting to believe him. "And you know what? I think it's time I told Ben Taylor that, the rat!"

She grabbed her purse and what was left of her sandwich and headed for the door, Gretchen hurrying along behind her.

"Well…I think you should probably call Joe first, before he hears about the obstetrician's office from someone else. You wouldn't want him to get the wrong idea," Gretchen said. She'd always had a soft spot for Joe.

Kate turned around, too mad to care about who knew what anymore. Her sisters' lease was signed. They were committed. They were moving in together.

"I don't care if Joe gets the wrong idea," she said. "He's in love with someone else."

She was still mad when she found Ben's church, an old monstrosity made of heavy, cut stone, faded with time, and huge, beautiful, stained-glass windows.

She charged into a room marked office, startling a very stern, disapproving-looking older woman who said imperially, "May I help you, young lady?"

"Ben Taylor. Where is he?"

"I'm not sure at the moment. He has an unfortunate habit of wandering away when my back is turned. What's he done now?"

Supposedly gotten me pregnant, Kate nearly said, then struggled to hold back a laugh at the expression that was likely to bring to the face of Ben's taskmaster. It would almost be worth it to say it, just to give Ben a taste of what she'd had to deal with already with

Gretchen and what was sure to come, as the gossip spread.

"I'm sorry. It's been a bad day. I'm normally never rude. Could you just tell me where he is?" Kate said. "Or…give me your best guess?"

She could imagine how the man would be hard to keep track of and sympathized completely with the older woman, who looked like somebody's grand-mother. Not the cuddly kind, but the kind people obeyed without question and every now and then, scared them half to death.

"The sink in the kitchen in the church hall has been acting up. I wouldn't be surprised if he was trying to fix it himself to save the money a plumber would charge us. He has no sense of decorum."

Kate's lips twitched in amusement once again, then realized that last bit about decorum could have easily been something she said about Ben.

What she as uptight and humorless as Ben's secre-tary?

"I'm going to find him. Do you want me to give him a message for you, if I do?"

"Yes, tell him I know he's not that forgetful and it's cowardly to sneak out without telling me where he's going, and there's no room for cowards in his profes-sion."

"Yes, ma'am." She could enjoy delivering that message.

She found the church hall, and sure enough, there with his head under the sink, nothing but his jean-clad legs and T-shirt-clad torso sticking out, was, she was sure, Ben Taylor.

"So," she said, standing five feet away and glaring at the spot where his head should be in about five seconds, "there's a rumor going around town that a certain member of the clergy has gotten me with child. You!"

She heard what she thought was his head thud against something solid, probably a pipe, and he might have said a bad word. She couldn't be sure, because he bit off the last part with a grimace as his head finally emerged from under the sink.

"Had to check and make sure who I was?" Kate asked.

"It would be a miracle along the lines of the immaculate conception for me to have gotten anybody pregnant, so I'm not really worried."

"You should be," she said, because he was grinning again, and she was mad. "It's not funny!"

"It is considering how close I've gotten to any women in the last two years."

"Well, I don't think it's funny. Not at all."

He sat on the floor wiping his hands on a towel then pushed his tools aside and got to his feet. "I don't suppose we could discuss this rationally?"

He was taller than Kate realized, and he wasn't wearing a T-shirt. It was…maybe an undershirt, but a skimpy one. A most un-clerical one. Torso-hugging and sleeveless, it showed off his shoulders and arms, looked just right with a pair of well-worn, black jeans.

Kate almost forgot she was mad for a moment.

"I am completely rational," she claimed, once she'd managed to stop looking at him that way. "I am never less than rational, not at any time in my life."

"Could we discuss this calmly?" he tried.

"I'm calm, I'm just furious. There's a difference."

"Okay," he said, good-naturedly. "Who says I knocked you up?"

And he looked like a guy completely capable of knocking up a woman, which wasn't helping her mood at all.

"Probably half the town by now. They saw us in Dr. Russell's office, and since Shannon didn't want to be seen with us, we sat there by ourselves looking like a couple." A bickering couple, if she recalled correctly. She hadn't been happy there, either, because of the delay and…well, she wasn't sure what. The prospect of living alone, maybe, for the first time in her life—assuming she could get Shannon out—and being seen in public with Ben and Shannon in full-dress black, plus having an ex-fiancé who was in love with someone else was enough to put any woman in a bad mood.

"So, we can't be seen in public without people thinking I got you pregnant?" Ben tried.

"Not in an obstetrician's office! And not when any friend of Melanie Mann is present."

"Oh. She is getting to be a problem. I don't suppose it occurred to you that I'm really not responsible for every piece of gossip that floats around this town?"

"When it comes to gossip about me, you seem to be." It was unfair, Kate knew, but she was still mad, and the idea of her, smart, responsible Kate, getting herself pregnant by a minister, while she was engaged to Joe, it was ludicrous!

"Well, what would you like me to do? I guess I could make an announcement from the pulpit on Sunday and swear that you're not pregnant, and that even if you were, it couldn't be my baby."

Kate's mouth dropped open, fury leaving her absolutely speechless.

"Okay, you're right," he said. "That's not going to

work. Plus, it makes me look like a cad. And I may be many things, but not that. If you were pregnant, I would stand by you every minute of the way."

Kate might have screamed at him herself, but from somewhere behind her she heard a gasp.

They both whirled around to see a delivery person holding an overnight envelope and a clipboard, glancing back and forth from Kate to Ben, finally sticking with Ben and saying, "Pastor Taylor?"

Ben nodded.

"Next-day letter for you. Could I get you to sign?"

"Sure." Ben signed, took the letter and thanked the man, then looked to Kate. "I guess you know him, too?"

Kate felt about a thousand years old. Everything just kept getting worse, no matter what she did. It just got worse.

"I think that guy played football at the high school when I was there. I think he's one of Melanie's old boyfriends."

Perfect.

"So…that probably didn't do our situation any good, huh?"

Kate shook her head. She was sure, if they looked out into the parking lot, the guy would be on his cell phone right then, calling Melanie.

"I think I'll go back to work now," Kate said.

She had appointments, she thought. Honestly, she couldn't remember. And she'd long since lost her list. What was she supposed to do today? A few important things, she knew. She just couldn't recall what they were.

But the phone would be ringing off the hook from the gossip. Gretchen would be hyperventilating, and

Kate really needed to be there, to figure out what she was going to say. People would be staring at her tummy for months, wondering, despite anything she said on the subject. And it would just get worse, once the news was out that she and Joe weren't engaged anymore. They'd all think it was because of her, because she'd gone and gotten pregnant by another man.

"I don't think I can do this anymore," she said, then frowned up at the man she'd still like to blame for all her problems.

"Do what?" he asked, too kindly for the way she'd attacked him.

"Anything." She feared she sounded like someone who'd just woken up from a three-year nap. Or a coma, maybe. What day was it? What had happened to her nice, safe, predictable life? "I can't seem to fix anything anymore."

"Well, what do you really need to fix today?"

Kate looked at him as though he'd absolutely lost his mind. "Oh, I don't know. Just about everything in my life!"

"No, you don't. You just need to go back to work. Take a few phone calls from busybodies. Say you've taken a pregnant teenager into your house and are just trying to get her a checkup. That you and I are working together to help her, not seeing each other socially. And then…go home. Take it easy. Take a bath or something. See a movie. Relax."

"I don't have time to relax! I don't have time for a movie!"

"Sure you do. You don't have to fix everything, Kate. You couldn't, even if you wanted to."

She felt the way she would if someone had told her the world had stopped rotating on its axis. What was wrong with this man? He was infuriating. Although…it did seem like she couldn't fix anything lately. And the whole idea that she wouldn't ever be able to again, that her whole life would deteriorate into a condition of complete chaos… God, that was terrifying. How could she live like that? How could anyone?

She wanted to cry again for about the sixteenth time in forty-eight hours. "I hate this," she whispered.

"I know."

And then he was right beside her somehow, big and solid and calm as could be. How did he manage that? It wasn't normal to be so calm or so good-natured, so willing to accept the crazy things that happened in life.

He pulled her close for a moment, warm and reassuring, kissed her forehead in a way that was sweet… Since when did she like anything that was sweet? She didn't even like chocolate, not really, not the way most women did.

And then he backed away, as if he expected her to come buzzing at him like a big, nasty bee and sting him.

All because he was nice to her.

Tears flooded her eyes then.

"I feel just awful," she said.

He felt her forehead, smiled a little. "No fever. You don't sound all stuffed up or like you have a scratchy throat."

"Not that way," she said, but he knew that. He was trying to cheer her up, maybe make her laugh. Why would he care if she laughed on a lousy day like this? "This was supposed to be a good day. A normal one. I had a list. I was going to handle everything."

"Yeah, that happens to me all the time. That stuff-not-working-out-as-planned thing. How about this?" he suggested. "Why don't you let me try to take care of this pregnancy rumor?"

"I take care of myself," she insisted.

"Just give this a try. Let someone else do it. Let me. Think of it as a character-building exercise. You're very task-oriented. I'm sure you like those."

"You're making fun of me," she complained.

"I'm trying to help you, Kate. Do you always make it this hard for people to help you?"

"Maybe."

"Like Shannon. You two are very alike, aside from your fashion sense."

"There's nothing wrong with my fashion sense," she insisted.

"I didn't say there was."

"And there's definitely something wrong with hers. I offered to take her shopping tonight, to pick up a few things for her, and she thought I wanted her to help me with my wardrobe! Like I'm going to start wearing black leather and chains!"

Ben laughed out loud at that.

Kate just felt tired. All of a sudden, she was so tired.

"Go home, Kate."

"I can't. I have to work."

"Then go to work. I'll call you and Shannon tonight and let you know if I've made any progress."

Which sounded a lot like letting him take care of her, something she'd never let anyone do.

Ben stood there watching her go. He'd never imagined her so sad. A little uptight, maybe, a little tense, a little too driven, but not sad, not defeated.

He shook his head. He was supposed to know how to help people, not drive them crazy. He walked back to his office, wondering at the last minute just how much Mrs. Ryan knew about the situation.

"You got that nice Cassidy girl pregnant?" she said, the minute he walked in.

"No," he responded, grabbing his black shirt and putting it on.

"You'd better not have! Because, I'd have to call someone at the diocese—"

"I didn't get her pregnant. I've never gotten anybody pregnant. At the rate I'm going, I never will."

"You don't have to shout about it," she reminded him, turning all prim and librarianish.

"Sorry. I'm going out for a while."

"Oh, no. Do you really think that's wise?"

"Probably not, but I'm going anyway." He put his white collar back on, thinking it might come in handy, and grabbed his keys.

"Where are you going?"

"Believe me, you don't want to know."

Chapter Nine

He stalked over to the Big Brothers/Big Sisters office, contemplating defrockment once again. At least it wasn't a violation of the law. He wouldn't go to jail. Mrs. Ryan would get a new boss, maybe one she approved of, and maybe the new guy could actually help some of the people of the parish. That would be a good thing.

Ben would go hide, far away from anyone, where he couldn't cause any harm.

There, he had a plan.

Kate would be happy, at least.

Maybe she'd make him a nice list, step-by-step, explaining everything very carefully, so that even he couldn't mess it up.

He trudged down the street, wondering how things had gotten so messed up so quickly. Wasn't it just three days ago he'd been here, all ready to help Shannon?

He pulled open the office door to find Melanie at her

desk, on the phone, whispering furiously. When she spotted him, she shut up right away, her mouth just falling open, no sound coming out.

Ben knew exactly what she was up to. He took the phone from her hand, said to the caller, "She's going to need to call you back," then hung up before anyone could say anything else.

Melanie gaped at him. "Is there a problem?"

"I think you know what the problem is," he said, making himself as big and intimidating as possible. It wasn't his best thing—intimidation—but he'd give it his best shot, for Kate's sake.

Melanie withered before him, managing to look about ten years old and innocent as could be, though he knew she wasn't.

Still…he really wasn't good at yelling or scaring people. There were more than enough you're-going-to-hell ministers in the world already. He'd always left it to them to scare people. He was more the can't-we-all-be-nice-to-one-another guys.

Okay, he could go with that.

Melanie wasn't being nice.

He sat down on the corner of her desk, made himself comfortable and found his best explain-things-to-little-children voice, since she was working hard to look like one.

"You know," he said. "There are people in this world who believe if you put nothing but good into the world, you'll get a lot of good back. I'm not sure if I'd go that far, because I've seen a lot of good people have lousy things happen to them."

Melanie nodded, eager to please, it seemed.

"But who knows? I don't have all the answers. I don't think anyone does."

"Me, neither," Melanie whispered.

"And those people also believe, if you do nothing but hurt people, maybe spread rumors about them and make them cry, there's a whole, big, blob of hurt, floating around the world with your name on it. That if you put it out there, you're going to get it back."

Melanie drew back as far as her chair allowed. Her lower lip started to quiver.

"Like I said, I'm not sure if I believe that entirely, but if I was somebody who acted like that, I think I'd be scared about what was coming to me, you know?"

"Well…" she began, but Ben was having none of that.

"And one thing you might have forgotten is that you had a fifteen-year-old girl come here a few days ago, all in black, looking as if she was dressed up for Halloween. Shannon Delaney, remember?"

"I think so."

"Maybe you didn't realize that I'm the one who got Shannon into this program. Because she came to me, at my church, for help, and I'm trying to help her."

"Oh," Melanie said.

"You might not know, either, that Kate is Shannon's big sister now, which means Kate's trying to help her, too."

"Yeah," Melanie said. "I knew that."

"And the biggest thing you might not know is that Shannon happens to be pregnant. She's been too scared to tell anyone, so she hasn't seen a doctor at all, which is really not good for her or the baby."

"Oh, no. It's not. I know that."

"So, you have two people trying to help Shannon. Doesn't it seem like one of the first things they'd do," Ben said, shouting at the end, "is take her to the doctor?"

Melanie's eyes got big and round, and as he yelled, she yelped, "Oh!"

"Yes, 'oh.' A doctor whose business is taking care of pregnant women. Maybe...Dr. Russell?"

Melanie nodded furiously.

"So, now you know what's going on. And if anyone came to you with questions about this, you could set them straight, right?"

"Yes."

"Wouldn't want anyone to get the wrong idea, right?"

"Right."

"In fact, you'd be doing a good thing, if you set a few people straight about this. I mean, if you happened to know people who might be...confused about it?"

"I could do that," she said.

"Good," he said, altogether pleased with his big, bad, intimidating man routine. "I think that's what you should do."

He picked up the phone he'd grabbed only moments ago, put it in her hand and waited for her to dial.

Gretchen gave Kate funny looks all afternoon, but Kate was determined to ignore them and all calls from anyone she was related to. She did her work, kind of, and tried to put together a plan that would get her sisters into their new apartment as soon as possible. This weekend, hopefully. That would be good.

Maybe she wouldn't have to tell them about her and Joe until they'd actually moved. That would be even better.

The clock said five o'clock, and Kate, who never left at five, found herself wanting to escape.

Go ahead, a little voice inside said. *There's no law that says you can't leave at five, even if you are the boss.*

Hmm. She supposed there wasn't.

Gretchen would be shocked and even more curious, but some things couldn't be helped. Kate shut off her computer, grabbed her satchel and her keys. She was halfway out the front door before Gretchen even realized what was going on.

"I'm taking off for the day," Kate said. "Will you lock up?"

Gretchen frowned, as if Kate had spoken in Swahili or something. "But…"

"Sorry, gotta go."

There it was.

She'd escaped.

Kate felt naughty and relieved at the same time, maybe something close to happy. And she was hungry. She'd been too upset to eat much that day. Suddenly her stomach was growling. She swung by the grocery store, whipping through like a woman who thought a grocery cart was a stock car in disguise, almost sending two unsuspecting shoppers barreling into displays, but causing no real disasters.

She got to the checkout lane and realized she'd bought nothing but ice cream and hamburgers to put on the grill. Kate frowned. Not the most nutritious dinner, especially for a woman carrying a baby, but there was protein in the burger and the ice cream had calcium, didn't it? She'd do better tomorrow. She'd take Shannon out to eat at someplace extra nutritious to make up for it.

She was zipping along the road to her house when she heard sirens behind her. Good grief! How fast was she going?

Glancing in her rearview mirror, she saw someone she hoped was her brother, then hoped it wasn't. She'd rather have a ticket than have to talk to anyone she knew right now.

Still, sirens were sirens.

She pulled over less than a block from her house, thinking if working up tears could get her out of this, it wouldn't be too hard at the moment. Glancing back, she saw it was indeed her big brother, Jax, climbing out of the car. *Great.*

"I cannot believe this." He talked as he walked to her car. "My sister would never break a rule, not even one about speeding. And yet, you look exactly like my sister. I can't be sure, because I didn't run the plates, but this looks just like her car."

"Just write me the ticket and be done with it," Kate said.

"Hey, you sound just like her, too," he said.

"Smart-ass," she mumbled.

"Oooohh, but she doesn't swear. That does it. You must not be her. Got some ID, lady?"

"Jax!"

"Of course…maybe…" He felt her forehead next, then frowned. "Wow. No fever. I thought you might be delirious and racing to the hospital."

"I am not delirious. I've never been delirious in my life. I'm just mad."

"Want me to go beat somebody up for you?"

He could do it, too. He was a thoroughly fine example of manhood, just turned thirty and more gorgeous than any creature had the right to be. Women flocked to him like bees to honey, and had his entire life—something he'd always accepted as simply the way of the world. He wasn't stuck-up, just very, very happy with his life. Tall, muscular and supremely confident, he could have taken care of anyone she asked him to with no problem.

Melanie Mann came to mind, but Jax would never hit a woman.

"Maybe…your fiancé?" he suggested.

"No."

"Well, if it's not him, the only other possibility I know about is this mysterious priest you're hanging out with, but honestly? My sister and a priest? No way. You'd be in major rule-breaking territory then."

"He's not a priest," she informed him. "And I'll have you know, I broke a rule yesterday, and I just broke another one today. I was speeding. Write me a ticket!"

"What did you do yesterday, Katie?"

"I didn't get pregnant, if that's what you're asking. Not that you have any room to talk, the way you've flitted from one woman to another your whole life—"

"Hey, I never—"

"Which has got to be an absolute miracle, considering all the girls you ran around with."

"And this isn't about me, anyway. This is about you. What's going on?"

"I…I…" She got distracted by a car driving past her at superslow speed. Someone's grandma. Maybe her best friend from third grade's or someone she babysat for when she was twelve. The woman gawked at Kate, wrinkling up her nose and squinting to get a better view, maybe.

Add one more thing to the growing list of gossip about Kate.

Now they'd probably say she'd been arrested for something.

"Come on. Tell me," her brother said. "And maybe

I can head off Kimmie and Kathie before they swoop down and demand to know everything."

"Oh, please, Jax. Don't let them do that."

"Tell me," he said.

"Okay, but…this is not an announcement for the general public or even the family yet, okay?"

"As long as I get to know, okay."

"Joe's in love with someone else," she said.

Her brother's expression grew thunderous. "He is not!"

"Yes, he is. He just told me."

"And you don't want me to go beat the crap out of him?"

"No, I just want to forget all about it. I didn't want to marry him, anyway."

"Oh," he said, more calmly than she would have believed.

Kate stared at him, dumbfounded. "What do you mean, 'Oh'?"

He shrugged, as if he'd told her Mrs. Barnes had lost her cat again, or that Mildred Lake had wandered away from the old folks' home once more and been found in a bar on Twelfth Street. Stuff that happened all the time.

"What do you mean, 'Oh'?" she said again.

"I mean, it's been five years, Katie."

"So?"

"Five years?"

He said it like that was a bad thing. "We were being careful. I'm a careful woman. You know that."

"Still, there's careful and then there's—"

Kate's mouth dropped open, making it hard to talk. "What?

"I don't know. Denial, maybe?"

Kate gasped. She was so mad she could spit. She absolutely couldn't believe this, not in a million years. "You mean...you knew?"

How could he know? She hadn't even known herself.

He shrugged helplessly. Her older brother was never helpless.

"All this time you knew?"

"Well...yeah," he said sheepishly.

"And you didn't tell me?"

"Katie, nobody can tell you anything."

Which very nearly made her cry. He didn't say it to be mean. He said it because it was true. She knew that. Just as she'd thought she'd known she was in love with Joe. But if she'd been wrong about that one important thing, what did it say about everything else she was so sure of? She really was going to cry.

"Oh, hell," her brother said, opening her car door. "Scoot over."

He slid in beside her. Next thing she knew, his arm was around her shoulder, and she was sobbing, her face hidden in his shirt.

"Ahhh, baby, I'm sorry. That rat. He didn't have to do it this way."

"It's awful! I never thought he'd do anything like this to me. I thought he was the safest man in the world for me, and he'd never leave me and never hurt me, and I would be as safe as I could be with him. That's why I picked him." Why in the world he'd picked her, she had no idea, but obviously he'd thought better of it.

Kate sobbed like she hadn't since their mother died.

"I'm sorry," Jax said gently. "I'm so, so sorry."

"And..." Kate sniffled, tried to stop crying, but couldn't. "And...I miss Mom!"

* * *

Jax followed her all the way home, pulling into the driveway behind her and walking to the door with her.

"Do I look just awful?" she asked, wiping at her face to make sure all her tears were gone before she walked in the front door.

"No."

She knew he was lying and loved him for it. He really was the sweetest thing to all of them, always had been, and it couldn't have been easy being the older brother to three lost little girls who hadn't had a father for most of their lives, being the man of the family from the time he was only eleven. They'd gotten through it together, as they'd done everything else, and the ties between them had grown stronger. She was lucky to have him. They all were.

He was about to open her front door when she stopped him with a hand on his arm. "I've been driving you all crazy, haven't I? Ever since mom got sick again."

"No," he lied again, just to make her not feel so bad.

"Yes, I have. And Joe, too. I could see myself doing it, and I just couldn't stop myself. I wonder if that's when he found this other woman…?"

"Katie, don't do this to yourself."

"I don't blame him. Not really. I'm not the easiest woman in the world to put up with," she said, then thought about it again. "Okay, I blame him a little."

"Me, too." Jax said. "In fact, I blame him a lot. All he had to say was, *I'm sorry, I don't want to marry you,* and walk away. That's it. Then he could have anybody he wanted and I'd be fine with it. I just hate that he did it this way."

"But not that he did it," Kate said. "Not if we're not supposed to be together."

"You would have figured it out," he said.

God, she felt so stupid. So incredibly stupid, and she'd always thought of herself as such an intelligent woman. How had this happened?

"Come on. You've got to face them sometime," Jax said. "And I'm here now. I'll run interference for you."

Which meant, if it got too intense, he'd run everybody off, if that's what she wanted. He was a good brother.

He opened the door. Looking inside, she saw her sisters in the kitchen, whispering furiously to each other. They stopped the instant they saw her. She'd expected time to pull herself together and think of what she was going to say, but she didn't get it.

Kathie walked up to her, a look of disbelief on her face and maybe a hint of anger, and said, "You're pregnant, and it's not even Joe's baby?"

"No!" Kate shouted.

"How could you do that to him? Poor Joe—"

"I didn't. I'm not pregnant."

"But you're running around town with somebody else. Everybody's seen you. Poor Joe—"

"There's no poor Joe in this," Kate said. "He's not the victim."

"He must be devastated," Kathie said, near tears.

"Trust me. He's not."

"Kathie, wait a minute." Jax stepped between them, as he so often had when they were little.

"She broke his heart," Kathie said.

"No, I didn't," Kate insisted.

Kim did her part, putting an arm around Kathie's shoulders and hanging on to her. "Wait. Give her a minute. Let her tell us what's going on."

"I know what's going on. I heard all about it."

"Well, you heard wrong, Kath," Jax said. "Joe left her."

"What?"

"He did," Kate said. "He's... Well, he says he's in love with someone else."

Kathie looked shocked.

Kim looked furious. "That rat!"

Kate wasn't up to going through the whole thing again. She was exhausted and turned to her brother. "You do it. I'm hiding in my room."

She didn't care if it was childish. And she still wanted her mother!

Kate, Ben and Shannon tromped into Dr. Russell's office together that morning in complete silence.

Once again Shannon was looking ghoulish and once again the poor mothers-to-be in the waiting room recoiled in abject terror when they saw her.

Kate started to laugh. She couldn't help it.

Ben checked in with the receptionist. Shannon, no doubt, meant to find a seat as far from the two of them as possible, but must have thought Kate was losing it when she'd started laughing to herself. She gave Kate a funny look, then sat down beside her.

Ben, looking uneasy himself, sat down at Kate's other side and said, "What?"

Shannon shrugged. "No idea. I didn't say a thing, I swear."

"What?" Kate giggled some more. Everyone was staring now. What would the local gossip have to say about this? That she was really losing it? "I think of funny things sometimes. I'm not completely humorless."

Was she?

Oh, geez.

Maybe she was.

Shannon rolled her eyes as the nurse called her name, stood up and stalked away. Kate got to her feet, then looked at Ben who hadn't.

"What?" he said. "I'm staying right here."

"No, you're not. You got me into this. You're not deserting us now."

"But it's a doctor. He's going to do... I don't even know what he's going to do back there. Women stuff."

"I would hope so."

"I'm not going back there," he argued.

"Yes, you are. You can guard the door and make sure Shannon doesn't disappear before she gets checked out."

He went reluctantly, but he went.

The nurse stopped at a wide spot in the hall, took Shannon's blood pressure, her temperature and pricked her finger.

"Ouch," Shannon complained.

The nurse shot Kate a look that clearly said, *If she thinks this hurts, just wait.*

Kate didn't want to think about that. Obviously, Ben didn't, either. Kate wasn't sure, but she thought he looked a bit pale at the sight of three drops of blood that had come out of Shannon's finger.

She was starting to feel a little nervous herself.

It all seemed too real now. There were huge, pregnant bellies everywhere. On posters on the wall and on the women sitting in the waiting room. Pictures of babies and a real baby or two, gurgling and waving their fists in the air, pulling their mother's hair and babbling as if they were carrying on a perfectly reasonable conversation, even if no one knew what they were saying.

Shannon, this poor lost little girl, was going to have a baby, and she had no one to help her through it, except Kate and Ben, and what did either of them know?

"Do you know anything about babies?" she whispered to him.

"They cry a lot and make messes," he said.

"Oh, great. You're going to be so helpful."

"You have two younger sisters. Don't you remember anything?"

"They cry and make messes," she said. "Sometimes, they smell really awful, and if they spit up on you, it's almost impossible to get the smell out."

"Out of you, or your clothes?" he asked.

"Both, I think."

He made a face.

What had they gotten themselves into?

The nurse was going to leave Kate and Ben on a sofa in the hallway outside the treatment room where they put Shannon. The girl looked pleadingly at Kate when it was time for her to go inside. She'd probably never had a pelvic exam, Kate realized, and wasn't that a treat for women everywhere.

"Okay, I'll go with you," Kate said.

Ben looked cheerful enough that she wanted to hit him, but held back.

"It was a man who got her into this condition," Kate said. "And where is he now? Nowhere to be found."

"Amen to that," the nurse said, as she held open the door, ushering them inside. "Cowards, nearly every one of them."

"Hey, I didn't do anything here. I'm just trying to help," Ben said.

"Cowards," the nurse repeated.

* * *

Ben sat there for twenty minutes, thinking things must have been going okay. Shannon hadn't tried to escape. He hadn't heard her so much as raise her voice. Then a nurse wheeled a big machine into the treatment room and he started to worry. What did that thing do? And what did they need it for?

He was thinking dire things when Kate stuck her head out the door a minute later and said, "Your turn."

"My turn for what?"

"Get in here."

He felt all the blood in his body rush to his feet. His head started spinning. "Why?"

"There's something you need to see," the nurse, who'd called him and all mankind a coward, yelled from behind the door.

"I don't think so."

Kate grabbed him by the arm and pulled.

They had the machine pulled up right beside the exam table. Shannon looked about six years old, lying there in her paper gown and her made-up face. The only part of her of any size at all was her rounded belly, which they'd uncovered.

How had she hidden a belly of that size from all of them?

Not that it was huge. Nothing about her was huge. But the belly wasn't nearly as flat as he'd thought, given how she looked in her big, baggy clothes. He was starting to get a very bad feeling about how close she was to delivering this baby.

"Everything okay?" he asked.

"We're about to find out," the doctor said, not sounding worried at all.

Shannon looked terrified. "Can I leave now?"

"Not yet," the nurse said. "Almost done."

The doctor squirted some goo on her belly and turned on the machine, which now looked like a big computer screen.

"We're going to get pictures?" Ben asked.

"Yes, we are."

"Does it hurt?" Ben asked.

"No," the doctor claimed, but from Shannon's expression, Ben wasn't so sure.

The picture on the screen looked like a TV on total static one minute, and then the next…Ben saw something.

"There." The doctor pointed to a remarkably clear image of a tiny face. "There's your baby."

Shannon peered at it as she might something coming at her in the dark at night, as if she wasn't sure if it was going to hurt her or not. Kate looked troubled, herself, and Ben…well, Ben was just glad it seemed to have all its parts in the right places, given the fact that she hadn't had any prenatal care.

There was a little blinking light in the middle of its chest, like a cursor on a computer. "What's that?'

"Heartbeat," the doctor said.

"Wow." A beating heart? Who'd have thought he'd ever be looking at one of those?

"It's…big," Shannon said. "The baby, I mean."

"Yes, it is. I think you're further along than you realized," the doctor said.

"How far along?"

"Like eight weeks or so from having this baby."

Shannon's mouth dropped open and stayed there. Kate gasped.

Ben thought they had a lot of things to figure out and not much time to do it. "Is the baby healthy?"

"Looks great. We drew blood, and we'll need to see the results of that test before we know for sure. But from my exam and the ultrasound, it looks like you have a healthy baby."

"Thank God," Ben whispered.

"Amen to that," the nurse said, then looked at Shannon. "You, little girl, need to be eating better and getting lots of rest. Having a baby is not easy, especially for someone as young as you. You just remember, this baby is depending on you."

From the look on Shannon's face, Ben thought she understood. The baby was suddenly, undeniably real.

"Do you want to know if it's a girl or a boy?" the doctor asked.

"No." Then she whispered to Ben, "What am I gonna do?"

"We'll figure it out," Ben promised her.

Chapter Ten

If they'd been somber going in, it was nothing like when they were coming out.

Shannon looked deflated, like she'd shrunk three sizes, a shell of her former self. Ben supposed being confronted with irrefutable evidence that she was going to have a baby very soon would do that to a young girl.

Kate was scribbling furiously in a tiny notebook.

He thought she was making a list.

A very long list.

He knew she made a lot of those, and he knew why. He wondered if she did.

Ben drove them both back to Kate's house. Shannon got out of the car and went inside. Kate put away her list, but she hadn't made any move to go inside.

"I'm going to have to keep her, aren't I?" she said.

"You could," he said, as noncommittally as possible.

"She's eight weeks from giving birth. I can't kick her out now."

"Okay," Ben said.

"Do you agree with everything people say? If I'd said I was going to ship her off to the North Pole, would you have sat there with that blank look on your face and said, 'Okay'?"

He grinned, because this was the Kate he was comfortable with. A silent, brooding Kate truly worried him. "Part of my training was in counseling. Listening, trying to let people find their own answers in their own way, that sort of thing."

"So if I'd said I was going to ship her off to the North Pole—"

"You wouldn't do that, Kate."

"But if I tried—"

"You wouldn't."

She made a sound of disgust. "That's infuriating!"

"What is? Knowing you're the kind of person who wouldn't put a pregnant fifteen-year-old on the streets? Knowing you always try to do the right thing? Yeah, I can see where most people would find that insulting."

"No, that way you just sit there and accept everything. Let people say what they want and try to go along with it."

"You want me to try to talk you out of keeping her?"

"No!"

"Want me to try to talk you into attempting to get Joe back?" He sure hoped not.

"No!"

"Then what? Want me to tell you what to do?"

"I always try to tell people what do to. It's what I do," she said.

"I know. Why is it so awful that I don't?"

"Ahh!" she said again, as if she could cheerfully strangle him.

Maybe she really didn't like him. He had to at least consider the possibility. He could be driving her crazy, and not in a good way.

He fought to keep a grin off his face, because he knew that irritated her, too. "What?"

"I just don't know how you do it. You never seem to tell anybody what to do, and yet you get people to go along with what you want. I tell people what to do, and they don't listen. And I'm not even sure now that I should be. I'm thinking, in my whole life, maybe I shouldn't have tried to tell anybody what to do, because I can't even manage my own life, all of a sudden. I mean, I don't think it's all of a sudden. I think I just figured it out."

She got really quiet toward the end. And sad. Now she was staring at him, waiting…

"Was there a question in there? Because I'm not sure if I caught it."

"What if I've been doing everything all wrong?"

"I don't think you have."

"I was wrong about Joe."

He shrugged, wishing she wouldn't keep asking about Joe. He didn't want to talk about Joe anymore. He didn't want to give any advice to anyone about Joe.

"What's really bothering you, Kate? It goes beyond Joe."

"See, that's what I'm talking about. You don't tell anybody anything, and yet you manage to lead people to what they really need to talk about."

"That's my job," he said.

"Oh."

She got really quiet at that. He'd definitely said something wrong.

"Okay," she said. "I need to go."

She reached for the door handle, and he reached for her, wrapping his hand around her arm and pulling her back when she would have gotten out of the car.

"Okay, let's back up," he said. "Just so there's no confusion about this point. I'm not working here."

"Sure you are. You and I are trying to help Shannon, and that's work to you."

"But not with you. You're not work."

"You're with me because of Shannon. We're both trying to help Shannon."

Ben didn't really see that he had any choice in the matter.

He decided he had to kiss her.

He'd been wanting to for a long, long time, and it seemed the only way to convince her that his interest in her had nothing to do with his job.

"Kate?" he said very softly, putting his hand on her cheek and turning her face to his. "I'm not working right now."

"But—"

He didn't let her get another word out. He covered her mouth with his, and let his lips linger on hers. His hand tangled in her hair, and she kept trying to talk, halfhearted efforts he ignored, except they were so like her, he wanted to laugh.

Leave it to Kate to think she could talk herself into making sense of a kiss, to be trying to analyze it while it was still going on.

He pulled away, laughing softly, and she looked furious.

"What are you doing?" she asked.

"Come on, Kate. You know what I was doing. I like you. You know that. You've known it from the first ten minutes we spent together."

"That is not what we're doing. We're trying to help this girl. We're working together," she insisted.

"I told you. I'm not working right now."

"But…but—"

No doubt about it. He'd have to kiss her again.

Kate had a million protests in mind, but didn't utter a single one.

Not this time.

This time, she just sat there and let him kiss her, let herself think that it was nice to be kissed by him. She hadn't kissed another man in years, and maybe that's what it was. Maybe just that he was someone different, the first new man she'd kissed in a long time.

Maybe that was why she wanted to sit here and just…feel.

It felt good.

Very, very good.

Like she couldn't move, good. Like she didn't want to. That good. She'd just stay there and try to not even breathe, and maybe if she did, he'd keep on doing it.

There were men who kissed like they were going to devour a woman whole, whether she wanted them to or not, and then there were men, like him, who kissed a woman softly, sweetly, tantalizingly, like a whisper that kept saying, *Come closer. Closer. Closer still.* Kisses that made a woman feel like she'd never be able to get close enough. That she'd always be moving toward a man, never away. Like she could crawl into his arms and then maybe inside his body completely and still it wouldn't be close enough.

Kate wasn't sure, but she thought she might have crawled into Ben Taylor's lap at some point. She didn't think he'd done it himself, and when he finally pulled away and she opened her eyes, she was practically in his lap, and he looked very, very pleased with himself.

She was mortified.

Terrified.

Completely baffled.

And had a grip on his shirt as though she'd never let go. Her breathing was shallow and fast. Her heart was pounding as if something like a tornado had picked her up and spun her around, dropped her off in a parallel universe.

Looking at his face, she wondered just who in the world this man was.

She hadn't even known him until three days ago.

Kate shook her head to try to clear it. It didn't work.

"If you laugh, I swear, I'm going to smack you," she said, because he was getting ready to. She could tell. She knew that, after just three days. She'd known it in two.

His lips were twitching. He was fighting it and losing.

"Don't you dare," she warned.

"Okay. Don't hurt me."

"And don't make fun of me."

"I'm not. I'm enjoying you. Very much. Don't look at me like that's a bad thing."

"I'm sure it is." Somehow it had to be.

"Oh, Kate. Did you forget completely how to enjoy life?"

"That's what you're doing? Enjoying life?"

"I'm enjoying this. Being with you. Knowing that you're a completely free woman right now and that I

like you, and that just about anything could happen between us."

She puzzled over that. *Anything?* "I just got out of
a five-year engagement."

"I remember."

"I can't do this!" she said.

"Why not?"

"It was two days ago!"

"So?"

"I have to figure out what went wrong, to make sure
it doesn't happen again." Of course she did. That's
what a rational, careful, thinking woman would do,
and Kate was all of those things. She was almost sure
of it. Three days ago, she would have been absolutely
sure, but now she wasn't, because he was kissing her
and she liked it and didn't want it to end!

"You know what happened, Kate," he claimed.

Only then did she realized that she was still sitting
on his lap, in his car, in her driveway, for anyone to see!
She let go of his shirt, pushed away from him and slid
onto her own seat with every bit of dignity she could
muster, which wasn't much.

"Oh, right. I know. Well, if I know, then I'm sure you
know, too. So why don't you tell me what happened
with my engagement."

"You didn't love him," Ben said, maddeningly calm
and sure of himself. "And you're not upset he's gone.
You're relieved, because you know deep down it was
the right thing. You're not supposed to be with Joe."

"I am not relieved," she claimed. "I'm upset."

"You're upset because you picked the wrong guy
five years ago and then refused to see it, because staying with him was easier than admitting you made a
mistake."

Kate's mouth dropped open in outrage. It was a terrible thing to say, made even worse by the fact that she feared it was true and that she'd only been saved from making a huge mistake with Joe by him falling for someone else.

What if she had married him? It would have been a disaster. A much bigger one than staying engaged to the wrong man for years.

"I really hate it when you do that," she told Ben, this man she'd known for three whole days, versus Joe, whom she'd known for more than five years.

How had he gotten so far inside her head in three days? How had their lives become so caught up in each other's? How could she think she liked him so much? He made her crazy most of the time. Crazy, not in a good way.

"When I do what?" he asked.

"Tell the truth," she admitted. "Big ones. Big, personal, private truths.

He grinned, just a bit. "Bad habit of mine."

They sat there in silence for a moment, Kate completely perplexed.

"I used to know exactly what I wanted," she said quietly, with no heat at all. "At least, I thought I did."

"You will again."

He said it like a promise, as if he had complete faith in her, when she had none in herself. It was the most terrifying thing, not trusting herself.

He sat there looking completely calm, completely sure of himself and so inviting, it was all she could do not to crawl back into his arms and beg him to hold her. He'd do it if she asked. She knew it and didn't think she'd ever been so tempted in her entire life.

By the thought of a funny, irritating, kindhearted rock of a man holding her?

He reached out and touched her face, so softly. Ran his thumb down her cheek, toyed with her chin, came close enough to kiss her, but ended up doing nothing but nuzzling his cheek gently against hers and whispering in her ear.

"You'll figure it out," he promised.

Kate got out of the car and ran to the house.

She'd hoped for a few moments alone, but that wasn't going to happen.

She walked into her own house to find both her sisters, her brother's fiancée, Gwen, and Shannon all in her living room, yacking about something. Probably her, judging by the way they shut up the minute they spotted her.

"Hi," Kim called out with what she was sure was fake cheerfulness. "Gwen came by to meet Shannon."

"Hi, Gwen."

"Hi."

She was the last woman in the world Kate would have expected her brother to fall for, but fall for her, he had. She'd never really expected him to settle down, either, and he'd proven her wrong about that, too. The only thing about the whole idea that drove Kate crazy was that he'd found Gwen in the middle of losing their mother. That at a time when the rest of them had been miserable, her brother had found a kind of happiness Kate had begun to think would completely elude her.

It wasn't very nice of her. She wanted her brother to be happy. She'd just been so unhappy herself the last few months.

"Everything okay?" Kim asked.

"Sure," Kate lied.

"You don't look like everything's okay," Kim suggested.

"No, it's just… Well…" She was still in that parallel universe, it seemed. Still a bit dazed and not sure what had happened.

"Do you feel all right?" Gwen was coming toward her, ready to do that hand-on-the-forehead, mom-thing. As if that could diagnose just about anything. Her whole family seemed to think so.

Kate's mother had done that, too.

She'd really like to have her mother back right now.

Tears threatened once again.

"Dammit," Kate muttered.

Instantly she was surrounded by her sisters and Gwen, all fussing over her like she was some weak, fragile thing. It was so irritating. She'd never allow herself to be weak, and there was no use being fragile. The world was tough, and it didn't care if a woman was fragile. It tore into her all the same. So there was no point in it.

"What happened?" Kim asked.

"He…he…he kissed me!"

"Joe?" Kathie looked stunned. "Joe kissed you."

"No. Ben!"

"Ben?" Gwen asked. "Who's Ben?"

"The priest," Kim said.

"He's not a priest. He's just a…well, he is and he isn't," Kate said, fumbling badly. "It's okay that he kissed me. I mean…it's not okay."

"You mean, he like…attacked you?" Gwen asked.

"No!" Kate cried out. "I mean…he's not that kind of priest."

"You mean…a fake one? He impersonates a priest?"

"No. I'm explaining it all wrong." But then, how could she explain it right? She didn't understand it herself.

Then she glanced up and saw Shannon. Shannon who didn't look quite so ghoulish today. Her face wasn't as pale as usual, her lips not as red, and she was wearing a cotton shirt that was merely gray, not black. Kate hadn't really noticed the change before. She'd been too caught up trying not to look pregnant at Dr. Russell's office and trying not to look like a couple with Ben, so that maybe some of the gossip would die down. She was expecting Joe to call any minute and scream at her about making him feel bad for loving someone else when she was having the priest's illegitimate baby.

Shannon was laughing, much in the same way Ben did.

"What?" Kate asked.

"I thought my life was messed up, but you…" Shannon said. "You're helping me just so you can pick up a priest?"

"I'm not picking him up. He's picking me up. Or… he's trying to. I'm just there," she said, claiming the innocent-bystander defense for what had to be the first time in her life. She hadn't exactly been an innocent bystander when she climbed into his lap a moment ago. "I don't know what he's doing. I don't know what I'm doing, but we're both trying to help you, and believe me, you need help."

She finally closed her mouth and realized everyone in the room was staring at her as though she'd grown three heads or something.

"What?" she said.

"You," Kim said. "You said that you don't know what you're doing."

"I don't."

"You always know what you're doing."

"Well…I don't anymore," she cried.

* * *

Ben was feeling particularly pleased with himself by the time he got back to his office, something which made Mrs. Ryan even more suspicious than before. She squinted at him with her glasses on, as if that would help her see him better and maybe figure out what he was doing.

"You're up to something," she accused.

"Yes, I am," he said.

"You've been running around with that girl again."

"Yes, I have," he admitted, pleased as can be.

It wasn't the most conventional courtship, but so what? He wasn't good at conventional courtship. He'd just have to try it his own way.

"I think she likes me, too," he said. "And don't listen to anything anybody tells you. She's not pregnant."

Mrs. Ryan gasped. Maybe she hadn't heard that particular rumor yet.

"By the way," he asked, "do we have any couples in the parish who are trying to adopt right now?"

Mrs. Ryan's mouth was hanging open, but no sound was coming out.

Ben liked this. Maybe he could keep her speechless for a while. His life would be much easier if he didn't have to listen to her tell him everything he was doing wrong. Of course, it might be a problem at times like this, when he needed to know something.

"Well?" he tried.

"Two, at least," she said. "Why?"

"Because I might be able to help them."

After all, he was here to help people.

Kate finally calmed down enough to go to work. Not that she got anything done. Then she went and left early again, nearly making Gretchen fall out of her chair to try to run after Kate before she got away.

She got home to find Shannon sprawled out on the couch eating ice cream.

They really had to do something about the girl's diet.

"What's wrong now?" Shannon asked.

"Nothing," Kate said. Not really.

Her sisters were acting as if the end of the world was coming or something, all because Kate was a little confused. Surely she'd been confused before. But they'd gotten all their utility deposits paid and were supposed to have electricity, gas and water by the weekend, which meant they could move.

Hallelujah!

Time to move on. Kate hadn't managed to make a list today, but she did have a few things lined up in her head that she needed to take care of.

Shannon was next.

"Look, I've been thinking…" she began.

Shannon jumped up off the sofa and put on her most belligerent look. "I know. I've overstayed my welcome. I'll get my things and get out of here."

"No," Kate said. Did she really think Kate could kick her out? When she was nearly eight months pregnant? "I want you to stay."

"You mean…for a few days," the girl said. Looking like a girl at the moment, not a Halloween mannequin.

"I mean, until after the baby comes," Kate said. "Kathie's moving in with Kim, so you can have her old room."

Shannon stared at her as if there had to be a trick of some sort. "Why would you want me to stay here? You don't even like me."

"I don't dislike you. I just...don't understand you," Kate admitted. "You know...the way you don't understand me."

Shannon laughed. "I understand you just fine. Little Miss Perfect. It's not that hard to figure out. You've always done everything right your whole life. And you've always made everyone around you feel stupid and completely inadequate."

Kate didn't know what to say to that.

"So," Shannon went on, "how'd I do?"

"I...I never wanted to make anybody feel bad."

Shannon arched a brow, as if to say, *So what?*

Kate felt awful all over again. "I just thought, if I always did the right thing, maybe I could keep bad things from happening to me. That's all. It's the only way I knew to protect myself. Not that it's worked. But didn't you ever try to protect yourself, Shannon? Didn't you ever think, it was up to you? That you were the only one who could do it?"

Angry tears filled the girl's eyes, and Kate felt bad for making her cry. It seemed she was failing once again.

"What if you stay until you find somewhere else to go?" Kate tried. "And if that doesn't happen until after the baby comes, that's okay."

"You just want to look good to Ben," she claimed.

Kate went back to the way she'd handled Shannon that first day in the park.

"What if I do?" she said, as offhandedly as she could manage. "It works for both of us, right? You get a place to stay, and I get what I want. It's perfect."

Shannon shrugged once again. "I guess so."

"Good. That's what we'll do. We need to find you some dinner."

Shannon held up the carton of ice cream and her spoon.

"No," Kate said. "Not that."

Time to play mother. In a nicer way, she hoped.

Chapter Eleven

Shannon watched in awe that weekend as Kate's sister actually started moving out. Kate and Ben moved what little Shannon had into the empty bedroom, then produced an old bedroom set of Kate's mother's for Shannon to use.

It looked as though she really was going to get to stay, and this was the nicest place she'd ever lived. It was warm, and she had her own room. There was always food in the refrigerator, and nobody yelled at her, except when she tried to sneak a cigarette, which she'd now promised not to do. They didn't even seem too upset that she was pregnant. She wouldn't let herself believe they actually cared about her, but she didn't have to have someone to care about her.

She spent a good hour arranging things in her room the way she wanted them, then her stomach started growling. On her way to the kitchen, she found Kate and Ben in deep conversation in the living room.

When he saw her, Ben said, "Hey. Why don't you come sit down? We need to talk about some things."

Her first thought was a panicked, *I don't get to stay after all*? She barely managed not to ask.

"It's nothing bad," Ben said.

He really did seem incredibly kind at times. Lost at other times, but mostly kind.

Shannon sat down.

"We need to talk about your baby, Shannon," he said.

"What about it? Is something wrong with the baby?"

"No. Nothing's wrong with the baby," Ben said. "We mean…what are you going to do with this baby? It's coming soon. You have some decisions to make."

"Are you going to make me give it up?" Shannon asked.

"I'm not going to make you do anything," he claimed. "This is your baby. You have to decide what's best for it."

"Which isn't me, you mean."

"You're going to have to decide that for yourself," Kate said.

Shannon made a face. "Like you're not going to tell me what to do? You tell everybody what to do."

"I'm reforming," Kate claimed.

Shannon gave a sarcastic laugh at that.

"No one can make this decision for you," Ben said. "It has to be yours."

Shannon could tell it was all Kate could do not to rattle off all the reasons she had to give this baby up. Not that she needed Kate to tell her. She'd thought of all of them herself. But it was her baby. She'd never had anything that was truly her own before, and she knew what it was like to lose a mother. She hadn't cared so much about her own mother, who'd never really been a mother to her. But losing her grandmother...that had been awful.

Still, all the practical things about keeping it couldn't be ignored. She had no money, no place to stay after the baby came, no job, not even a high school diploma, and she'd lived with people who'd struggled with money their whole lives. Not struggled to afford a nice car or a nice house. Struggled to afford any car or any kind of place to live and to put food on the table. To have money to go to the doctor when they were sick. Things like that. She didn't want her baby to ever go hungry, to ever end up living on the streets or be sick and not be able to go see a doctor.

But wouldn't she find a way to keep her baby if she really loved it? Wasn't that what a mother did?

"Go ahead," Shannon said. "Tell me what you think I should do. I know you want to. I know you're going to, no matter what you say."

Kate opened her mouth to respond, but Ben put his hand out to stop her.

"All I want you to do is look at your options," he said.

"Which means...what?"

"I talked to your teacher, Betty. She knows four girls at your high school who had babies last year. I want you to talk to them and see what their lives are like now."

"So I'll think it's too hard and give up my baby?" she said.

"So you'll have a realistic idea of what you're getting into," he claimed. "Come on, Shannon. That's not too much to ask. I think you're a realist at heart. I think you want to know what it's going to be like."

She shrugged. Maybe she did, and maybe she didn't. "What else?"

"I have a number of couples who go to my church who've adopted. I want you to meet some of them, meet their children, see how that's working out for them."

"What else?" she asked.

"That's it. Just talk to some people. Surely that's not too much to ask."

He sounded as reasonable as always, and he did seem to be a really nice man, a good one, completely unlike her father or her ex-boyfriend, both of whom didn't want anything to do with her or her baby.

"Do you have kids?" she asked.

"No."

"You ever want them?"

"Someday."

She wouldn't mind so much giving her baby to him. She hadn't been sure men like him existed in the world, but here he was, seeming to be everything the males in her life weren't. He'd make a good father, she thought. He wouldn't yell. He wouldn't lose his temper. He'd probably always care.

"Just tell me you'll talk to them, Shannon," he said.

"All right."

She'd talk.

How hard could that be?

Kate made spaghetti for dinner, and she managed to stay quiet until Shannon went to take a shower before bed. The minute she heard the shower come on, she turned to Ben.

"What do you mean, you're not going to tell her what to do?"

"I'm not," he said, in the middle of clearing plates from the table. "I can't."

"Of course you can. You say, 'Shannon, you have no idea what it's going to take to raise this baby. You have to give it up.' How hard is that?"

"She won't do it because someone tells her to, Kate. And she won't believe me if I tell her she can't take care of her baby. She has to figure it out for herself."

"You're going to trust a fifteen-year-old to do that?" Kate asked, as she rinsed the dishes and handed them to him, to put in the dishwasher. It left them side by side in her kitchen, so close they hardly had to raise their voices to argue.

"I don't have a choice."

"That's right, because you don't tell people what to do. You just steer them toward the decision you want them to make, and it works for you? Well, she doesn't steer well."

"What else can I do? I'm not her father. I'm not her legal guardian. I'm not anything to her, except a guy who's trying to help. I can't make her do anything."

"Well, somebody has to," Kate argued as she dried her hands, dishes done.

"Fine, if you think you can do it, go ahead." He was practically yelling at her. "Let me know how it works."

Kate was surprised at the sharpness of his tone. He looked tired, she realized, as he stood there leaning slightly against her cabinets. He looked almost sad. She'd never seen him sad.

"Is something wrong?" she asked.

"Lots of things are terribly wrong in this world."

"Something in yours specifically right now?"

He groaned, more angrily than sad, and looked away. "Yeah."

"What is it?"

"Bad day at work," was all he said. "What about Shannon?"

"What about you?" A bad day at work for her was too many phone calls, documents missing, deadlines that no one cared about making but her. His bad days were likely much worse. "Mrs. Ryan catch you doing something you shouldn't?"

"No. Nothing like that."

Kate finally felt like she was getting her footing with him. So far, all he'd done was help her and Shannon, and Kate just didn't know how to let people help her. She wasn't comfortable with the idea. But her helping others…that was her forte. This was the way life was supposed to be.

"Come on." She took his hand and tugged until he followed her back to the sofa and sat down beside her. "Tell me. I can help."

"No, you can't."

"Sure. We'll make a list. Do you ever make lists? We'll break the problem down step by step and cross things off as we go. It'll be great, you'll see."

"A list isn't going to help, Kate."

"Sure it will. What's the problem?"

He looked her right in the eye, his expression as bleak as any she'd ever seen and said, "A young couple in my parish had a baby five months ago. Hannah. Gorgeous little thing with the most beautiful smile. She has a heart problem, something the doctors don't think they can fix. And…well, they didn't expect her to last this long, but she has, and now she's getting worse. I've been at the hospital most of the day with them. It's… it's hard."

"Oh." She backed away physically, her whole being

recoiling from the pain and the unfairness of it. "There's no list for that. I hate problems where there's no list that helps. I don't know how to deal with them."

"Yeah. There shouldn't be problems where a list won't help."

"Exactly," she said. "Is there anything I can do? Do they need anything?"

"Nothing anybody in this world can give them."

He said it with a kind of resignation that pulled at her heart. People came to him with unsolvable problems, she realized, and expected him to be able to help. What would that be like day in and day out? Having people bring unsolvable problems and expect him to fix them? Or make sense of them?

"Don't you get angry?" she asked.

"Very often."

"What do you do about it?"

"Get angry," he said. "What can I do? I'm just a man."

And yet, people wanted him to be more. She knew because she'd wanted the same thing from her mother's pastor when her mother lay dying and there was nothing to be done. She'd been so angry, had even taken some of it out on the minister, not her finest hour.

Kate took Ben's hand in hers and this time, held on to it. He looked up in surprise, with questions, it seemed. She ignored them and just sat there with him.

"And then, here's Shannon," she said, "having a baby when she's much too young to take care of one, with no one to help her, and this poor couple's probably going to lose their daughter... It doesn't make any sense. I meant to sign up for a world that made sense. Where actions had predictable consequences and somebody spelled out all the rules clearly, so people knew what to do to keep themselves safe. That's the world I wanted."

"The one with all the lists," he said, not looking quite so bleak.

"Yes. That one. Why couldn't it work like that? That would make sense."

He shook his head. "Don't know."

And then they sat there, quiet as could be. She held his hand and then eased over beside him and put her head on his shoulder, wishing she could take some of his pain and frustration away, wishing she knew something to say.

He'd been so good to Shannon and to Kate, and here she was, feeling like there was nothing she could say to make things any better for him.

They stayed that way for a long time before he got up to leave. She walked him to the door, and before he left, ended up wrapped up in his arms, kissing him softly, sweetly, kindly, wishing she could help him in the same way he'd helped her.

Kate was grabbing a quick lunch at the diner on the corner two days later when she came face-to-face with Joe.

"Hi." She felt every eye in the place turn to them.

They hadn't bumped into each other since their little talk about him being in love with someone else. He gave her an odd look, one that started at her face and ended pointedly at her waistline.

"No," she said, not quietly. "I'm not pregnant."

A collective gasp went through the diner, and Kate had to fight not to laugh. Might as well take care of that little rumor right then and there.

"Well, that's good to know," he said. "I hear you have a new…friend."

He made *friend* sound like a dirty word.

Kate laughed. "I do, but I'm not in love with him, the way you are with… I don't even know her name. What's her name, Joe? How long have you known her?"

Another collective gasp, this one even louder.

Joe's cheeks flushed an angry color of red, probably not so much because she'd been seen running around town with Ben, but because she'd made a scene. He hated any sort of public confrontation.

"Go ahead and ask," she told him. "Whatever you want to know, I'll tell you."

"Were you seeing someone else while we were together?" he whispered furiously.

"No. I wasn't. I met him the day before you and I broke up."

"Really?"

"Yes."

"All right." He nodded. "I'm sorry."

"Me, too." That they both hadn't handled this better. "I hope you'll be happy with this woman, whoever she is."

He shot her a look that she couldn't begin to understand. Like…she had no idea what he was facing? Or how little chance there was of him being happy? What in the world?

"You really mean that?" he asked.

"I do." She could never hate him. She could be angry for a while, and she was hurt, but she was as much to blame as he was, and she truly hoped his next relationship worked out better than theirs. Kate whispered, not angry any more and not interested in causing a scene, "She's not married, is she?"

"No!"

"Okay. Well…what is it?"

"I can't tell you."

"Well, tell her. I mean, if she's the one you really want, go get her," Kate said.

"It's not that simple."

"Sure it is. If you're in love with her, and she's in love with you—"

"I have no idea how she feels about me, and I hope she doesn't know how I feel about her."

"Joe, that's ridiculous. You don't stand a chance that way. You have to tell her how you feel." Kate remembered how bewildered he looked that first night when he'd told her. He seemed to be wishing every bit of emotion he had for this other woman would just magically disappear, so he and Kate could follow their nice, safe, little plan that wouldn't have worked for either of them.

"It would ruin everything if I told her," he claimed.

"That makes absolutely no sense. I've never heard you make such little sense before. Telling her is the only way it can work out between you. Unless you're waiting for her to just figure out how you feel and come throw herself at you."

"She's not going to do that."

"So…what? The two of you are just going to go on like this? Loving each other and being miserable and apart?"

"I don't know. I have absolutely no idea what to do. I've never felt like this in my life."

"Yeah…well, I know all about that."

She gave him a big hug and a kiss on the cheek, wondered if the gossips in town would have them back together by dinnertime, but just didn't care anymore. It was over. She knew it.

* * *

Ben got back from the hospital shortly after three that afternoon, and Mrs. Ryan was waiting for him. She had a cup of hot fresh coffee in one hand and a stack of messages in the other.

"No change in little Hannah?" she asked.

"Still hanging on." He took the messages. "Anything urgent here?"

"Two of those teenage moms called back. They're willing to meet with you and Shannon."

"Good." At least one thing was going okay.

"It was a good thing you did, chasing after her that way, helping her."

Ben thought he might have lost so much sleep he was hallucinating. Mrs. Ryan was complimenting him on something? "Are you feeling okay?"

"Don't be mean about it. When someone says something nice to you, the proper thing to do is to simply say, 'Thank you,'" she told him, her stern self back.

"Thank you, Mrs. Ryan. I mean that. Anything else?"

"Well…there is one thing, and I'm not sure how to tell you this. You know I'm not one for gossip…"

"Of course not." She was the soul of discretion.

"But…I thought you should know…that woman who's been helping you with Shannon? Kate Cassidy?"

"Yes. What about Kate?"

"Apparently, she and her fiancé ran into each other at the Corner Café today at lunch," Mrs. Ryan said, as if the whole thing was distasteful to her, to stoop so low as to gossip like that.

"And?" he prompted.

"Apparently, they're back together."

Ben frowned. "I don't think so."

"Apparently, they were seen…hugging and kissing in the diner today."

"I don't think so," Ben said again.

"I just thought I should warn you, because…well, you seem to have taken an interest in her, and I didn't want you to hear about it from someone else."

"You're afraid I'm going to get hurt?" he said, astonished. "You're worried about me?"

"I felt it was my duty to warn you. I didn't want you to be blindsided by small-minded people who have nothing better to do than spread malicious gossip."

"You are worried about me, which means you must like me just a little bit."

"Don't be ridiculous," she said, as primly as he'd ever heard her.

"I'm touched," he told her. "Honestly. I didn't think I'd ever do anything to make you like me."

"You still have a lot to learn about running a church."

"Of course. And I'm counting on you to teach me. And to keep me in line."

"I'll do my best," she promised.

Ben laughed. He didn't believe Kate and Joe had made up for a second, not given how wrong the gossips had been about him and Kate lately. Talked to each other, hugged, maybe even kissed good-bye, but not gotten back together.

Kate was going to be his.

Kate, Ben and Shannon went to visit Allison Grant the following Saturday. She'd just turned seventeen, was a high school junior and raising a little boy, Graham, who was eight months old.

Shannon looked nervous. Kate looked determined, probably to make Shannon see that she couldn't raise her baby on her own. She'd been talking about making pro-and-con lists while they were at Allison's house. Ben was tired, because he was still spending a lot of time at the hospital with baby Hannah and her parents, but happy to be taking this step with Shannon.

They found the house with no problem, then the apartment over the garage where Allison was living. It didn't look like much.

"What about her mother?" Shannon asked, as they got out of the car.

"Didn't want her to keep the baby, and when Allison did, she made Allison and the baby move out. I think she's still holding out hope that Allison will change her mind. The mother said she'd take Allison back if she gave up the baby."

"That's awful," Kate said, looking up at the garage apartment.

"The mother said she wasn't going to end up raising the baby for Allison."

"My mother would have probably done the same thing," Shannon said.

"Mine wouldn't have," Kate said. "She wouldn't have raised the baby herself. She would have made sure the baby's mother did that, but she would never have kicked us out of the house, either."

"She wouldn't have just ordered you to give up the baby," Ben whispered in Kate's ear.

She turned around and glared at him, and he laughed.

"Still think it would work?" he asked.

"I'm not speaking to you right now," she said.

Shannon turned around and gave them a funny look.

"What?" Kate said, as they climbed the rickety steps leading to the apartment.

"If you two want to go out or something, don't let me stop you."

"We're not going out," Kate said.

"So you're just going to keep flirting with him, but never do anything about it?"

"I'm not flirting with him!"

"Sure you are," Shannon said.

"I was really hoping you were," Ben added.

Shannon laughed.

Kate glared at him some more.

"You look so cute when you do that," Ben said.

"Do what?"

"Try to look intimidating and mad."

Kate rang the bell with more force than necessary. "I do not look cute. I look intimidating. I have a very intimidating look!"

"No, you don't," Shannon said. "You can look uptight like no one I've ever seen, but you can't do intimidating at all."

"I'll have you both know, there are people who live in fear of making me mad."

At which both Ben and Shannon broke out laughing.

Kate rang the bell again, not sure if she heard anything when she did, so she knocked instead, intent on ignoring her two companions.

"By the way, she's not getting back together with Joe," Shannon said. "No matter what you heard about them at the diner."

"I know," Ben said.

Which only made Kate even madder.

Shannon thought baby Graham was built like a barrel, short and stocky and round. He was strong as an ox, determined and simply would not listen to reason.

"You cannot have that," Shannon said, sitting on the floor to get at eye level with him, enunciating each word very carefully, as if that would help him understand. "You'll break it."

"Ahhhhuuuhhhh," he squealed, reaching for the phone, which he liked to bash against the coffee table, probably because he liked the noise it made.

"He's a complete barbarian," Kate said. "I don't remember my sisters being like this."

"Ahhhhuhhhhhuhhhhuhhh."

The sound came out like an angry wave. Big tears filled his pretty brown eyes and fell down his soft, baby cheeks. He was cute, but a lot of trouble and still greatly distressed over the phone thing.

Ben, that rat, had offered to let the mother go out for a few hours while they were here, and she'd jumped at the chance. Shannon was beginning to see why. When she thought of her baby, she pictured something cuddly and sweet, not strong and determined and nearly always mad.

Or maybe she was just doing it all wrong.

Maybe she didn't know what to do.

"Ahhhhhrrrrr," he squealed again.

"Keys?" Kate offered hers. There were about ten on the ring. She showed him how they jingled when she shook them.

He took them and promptly poked himself in the face with one, then started to cry. It left a big, red mark, which he obviously blamed Shannon for. He looked at her as if she was a monster and cried some more.

Kate looked horrified. Ben looked as if he wasn't too surprised at how this was working out.

"You're making this harder than it has to be," Shannon said.

"I don't have to make it hard. It is hard," he argued, sitting comfortably on the couch and letting her deal with everything. "And you need to know that."

"You want me to say I can't do it," she said nearly crying.

"No, I want you to know what you're getting into."

"He just doesn't like me. That's all."

"Fine. We'll go see a dozen babies to find out if any of them like you more than he does."

Graham was chewing on the edge of the coffee table now. Surely that wasn't good.

Shannon picked up his gushy, plasticlike ring and handed it to him. He sucked greedily, then started gumming it, drool leaking out of his mouth and onto his fingers, his sleeper, onto everything.

"Oh, gross," Shannon said.

"I'm sure that's not the grossest thing he can do," Ben said.

"Yeah, but I know there's more to it than this," Shannon said. "There are good things. Lots of them. I bet he loves his mother. I bet he's happy with her."

"Sometimes. But a lot of times, he's just like this," Ben said.

She and Kate had chased him all over the living room. He wasn't quite crawling, but he did this scooting thing, up on his arms and dragging the rest of his body, and managed to get around really well. Really fast.

He'd pulled a bunch of magazines down on his head and cried about it. He'd stood up and made his way around the coffee table, then fallen and banged his chin on it and cried more. He'd wanted to suck on Shannon's boots. The bottom of her boots! Gross!

He was always busy and never happy for long.

"It would be different with my baby," Shannon insisted.

Kate, now sitting comfortably in a chair, gave her a look that said, *Sure it would.*

Graham scooted over to Shannon and pulled himself up by hanging on to her shirt and arm. He patted her cheeks, kind of. Or maybe he was hitting her. She couldn't be sure. It didn't really hurt, but it didn't feel good.

Then he stuck his fingers into her mouth and said, "Bahhhhhhh."

"Yuck, Graham!"

He looked hurt.

He looked...odd.

Then he made a silly face and spit up on her.

It was all Shannon could do not to throw up herself.

"Well, I guess you think that went well," Kate said later, when they'd gotten back to her house and Shannon had gone to her room to get out of her smelly clothes and try to wash baby spit-up out of her hair, among other things.

Ben shrugged, not looking happy, just tired, resigned, maybe. "It had to be done."

"You think she'll meet with the adoptive parents now?"

Ben nodded.

Kate decided Ben could give lessons in getting people to do things they didn't want to do. He'd certainly gotten her to face up to her true feelings about Joe.

"About what Shannon said, I meant to tell you myself that if you should hear a rumor or two about me and Joe at the café last Monday..."

He grinned. "That you're getting back together?"

"Right. About that. Shannon was right. We're not."

He looked like he was waiting for something that was actually news. "Mrs. Ryan told me," he said.

"Mrs. Ryan gossips?"

"No. Never. She was just…looking out for me. We had a breakthrough. She's decided I'm not completely worthless."

"She was worried about you?" Kate realized. "Wow. That is a breakthrough. I just thought you'd want to hear it from me, that we weren't getting back together."

"I know," he insisted.

Kate put her hands on her hips. "Just like that? No doubts."

"None."

"Why not?"

"Because I know you, Kate. You hate to do the wrong thing, and going back to Joe would definitely be the wrong thing, and you know it." He came to her, put his hands on either side of her waist. "Besides, you like me."

She tilted her head up to look into his eyes. He was going to kiss her, and she was glad. "You're sure about that?"

"Positive."

"Anybody ever tell you that you have an arrogant streak, Reverend?"

"No."

"Because you look awfully sure of yourself."

"There's a difference between being sure of yourself and being arrogant. Although, I'm not quite sure what the difference is now." He paused, a millimeter away from her mouth. "Shut up and kiss me, Kate."

Chapter Twelve

Kate's smile was so big, she wasn't sure they could manage a kiss, but he made it work. She went eagerly into his arms, happy to wrap her arms around him and hold him close, to give herself up to this moment.

It was as if he wove a spell around them, pushing everything else away.

There was something about him, something very, very special.

He groaned and crushed her to him, his kisses like something she could happily drown in.

"You shouldn't be so good at this," she protested. "There's something decidedly unministerlike about it."

"I didn't go into the seminary until I was twenty-seven." He backed her up to the couch and eased her down. "I was just a regular guy. I'd kissed a few women by then."

"I'd say more than a few."

He sat down on the edge of the sofa and leaned over to kiss her. "It would be ungentlemanly of me to talk about it."

"And you would never be ungentlemanly."

"Well, I shouldn't be."

Kate pulled him down to her. She rolled onto her side, and he was on his side, facing her. It was close quarters, but she wanted to be close.

"So, what does a gentleman do in a situation like this?" she asked.

"Listens very carefully for the sound of the shower, so the teenager doesn't come out and find us like this," he said.

His mouth settled softly on the side of her neck. It tickled, and at the same time felt very, very good. She squirmed and laughed, wrapping her arms tightly around him, sheer joy filling up inside of her and spilling over.

She pressed her mouth to his, closed her eyes and simply enjoyed herself and the feel of his entire body pressed to hers. Her whole body was tingling and alive, hungry for him.

He kissed like a man who had all day to do it, like he could happily explore nothing but her mouth for ages and ages. Kate ran her hand through his hair, along the hard line of his jaw, holding him to her.

Nothing was going to happen, because Shannon was in the shower, which meant this was nothing more than an exploration of each other, an enjoyment.

Kate intended to enjoy it to the fullest. She wasn't worried about controlling it or analyzing it, just letting herself go with it.

He was nibbling on her ear, which made her squirm some more, trying to get away from him at the same time she was trying to get closer. He buried his head in the curve between her shoulder and her neck, and she gasped. There was something about that spot that just made her melt.

"Like that, huh?"

She nodded.

He used his teeth, gently but very effectively. She shivered and made a pitiful little begging sound that she knew he heard. She could feel him grinning against her neck.

"Oh, yeah. This is a good spot," he said, lifting his head just long enough to nudge the lapel of her blouse aside to find her collarbone. "I need to find every spot like that on your body."

Then he traced her collarbone with his tongue, nuzzled it with his nose.

She could feel what it was doing to his body and what this was doing to hers, and all she wanted to do was get closer to him.

Her breathing was labored, as was his.

"The shower's still going?" she asked.

"Still going. I'll listen. Don't worry."

"Okay."

Maybe she wouldn't worry about anything.

A woman could do that with him.

She felt perfectly safe with him, until she considered how much she wanted him and how fast it had all happened.

He just felt so good.

And he was so good to her.

His mouth was playing in that hollow at the base of her throat, and then at the back of her neck. It sent shivers all the way down her spine, all through her body.

Who'd have thought making out on her couch like teenagers could feel this good?

Kate pulled his mouth back to hers, feeling like they were both playing with fire at this point, but what did it matter? They weren't really going to do anything.

Kisses and kisses and more kisses, it wasn't going to go anywhere.

They both still had all their clothes on, and nothing was coming off.

Still, it felt naughty, like something she definitely wasn't supposed to do.

Kate was never naughty.

She kissed his gorgeous, generous mouth, his eyelids, his jaw and was teasing his ear when…

She heard something.

A gasp.

Ben looked down at her, puzzled.

"It wasn't me," she whispered.

He eased off her, and they both sat up, looking at the hallway that led to Shannon's room.

Nothing there.

Then, puzzled, they both turned the other way, toward the front door, and there was Kate's sister, Kathie.

"Oops," Kate said.

"I thought she'd moved out," Ben whispered, scrambling to his feet.

"She did. Kind of." Kate jumped up, too. "I mean… mostly. Just not completely. She still has some things here."

Kathie stared at them as if they were sixteen and she was their mother. "I thought you got back together with Joe at the diner?" she yelled.

"No," Kate said.

"Would you just make up your mind!"

"I have," Kate said. "I'm done with Joe."

"Did you tell him that?"

"Yes, I made it perfectly clear."

To which, her sister said nothing at all for the longest time.

She looked so upset, Kate didn't know what to make of it. "Are you all right?"

"I'm fine," Kathie said. "I'm just great. I'll come back for my things later, and I'll call first."

She was out the door before Kate could say anything else.

Kate turned back to Ben, wondering if he understood any better than she did, but before she could ask, she heard someone else behind them.

Shannon stood there in her flannel pajamas, her hair all wet, her expression one of sheer disgust.

"You guys want to get a room or something?" she suggested. "And try to use something more reliable than a condom. It didn't really work for me, and I'd hate to see you get spit up on on a regular basis by a pint-size barbarian."

Then she stormed off back into her bedroom.

Kate waited, to make sure no one else was going to show up and yell at them, then looked at Ben.

"So," he said. "That went well."

Kate tried to come up with some kind of look that spoke of both annoyance and some sense of enjoyment at the same time.

"You had a really boring life until a few weeks ago, didn't you?" he said.

"Yes, I did."

"But it's better now." He seemed very pleased by that.

Kate was, too, although she was in no hurry to tell him that. She folded her arms in front of her and said, "You're a very unusual man."

"Thank you."

"I don't even know if it was a compliment myself. How can you be so sure it is?"

"Because you like me. And I like you." He kissed the tip of her nose. "And because an ordinary man just wouldn't do for you, Kate."

Kate felt as though she'd gotten called into the principal's office five days later, when in reality, it was a summons to Charlotte Sims's office.

"So, how are things going with Shannon?" Charlotte asked.

"Fine."

"Because, I keep hearing things, Kate. Things about her maybe living at your house, and I have to tell you, that's just not what we do here. We're not supposed to become parents to these kids or guardians or anything like that."

"Oh. Okay." So, she'd definitely broken a rule.

"I mean, it's good that you care, and I know these kids need a lot more than we can provide at times. But to just take a child into your home…the child welfare department frowns on that. They have rules. They like to do things like home studies and check references and bring you into the foster care program, and we try to stay on their good side. So, if Shannon was living with you…"

Charlotte looked pointedly at her.

Was Kate supposed to confess? Or deny it all, because if Charlotte didn't know about it, Kate wasn't getting her in trouble, just herself, right?

She really wasn't sure, because she never broke rules.

"I'm…not really sure where Shannon is right now," she said.

It wasn't exactly a lie.

Shannon was supposed to be at school, but Kate already knew the girl had a habit of skipping. She could be anywhere.

"Okay," Charlotte said, taking a breath and letting it out slow. "But…you see her from time to time, and she seems all right?"

"Yes," Kate said. "We took her to the doctor. Ben and I—"

"Yes, I heard all about that."

"And her baby's coming soon. A month or so, the doctor thinks. We got her prenatal vitamins, and I got her some maternity clothes. Or…well, she hated all the maternity clothes. But we got her some stretchy pants and big tops to wear. And Ben's trying to help her figure out what to do once the baby comes. We're meeting with a couple who adopted a baby a year ago, so Shannon can see them together and hopefully see how well that can work out."

"Okay. Anything else you want to tell me?"

"No. Not really," Kate said. Was there something else she should say?

"Well. Great. Keep up the good work."

"We will," Kate promised.

She was out of the office in no time, thinking she really didn't care about rules. Shannon needed a place to stay and someone to take care of her right now, and Kate and Ben were doing that. Kate didn't care what the rules were!

She was grinning like crazy as she walked out of Charlotte's office and came face-to-face with Melanie Mann. She hadn't been at her desk when Kate had arrived, but now here she was, looking almost scared.

Of Kate?

"Hi," she said tentatively.

"Hi," Kate said.

Melanie just looked at her, as if she was ready to get yelled at.

Kate couldn't think of why, and she really didn't care that Melanie was the biggest gossip in the world. In fact, she thought it could come in handy. Kate was tired of all the gossip about her and Joe, the on-again, off-again stuff. It was ridiculous. She could clear that all up right now.

"Melanie? Joe and I are done," Kate said. "For good. That little scene in the café…I was just wishing him well. We're not getting back together. Not ever. Understand?"

Melanie nodded.

"Spread it around, okay?" Kate said.

She thought she must be wrong, but she could swear Melanie looked more scared than ever. How odd.

That weekend Kate, Ben and Shannon visited a couple in Ben's parish who'd adopted a little girl the year before. She was almost fifteen months old, walking like she was half-drunk, babbling constantly and drooling even more than baby Graham had been.

But she looked very, very happy and absolutely at home with her adoptive parents, Tim and Tina Richardson. They were the cutest couple, high school sweethearts, they said. She was a secretary, and he was an engineer. They'd spent ten years trying unsuccessfully to have a baby before they managed to adopt baby Emily.

She was doing her drunken-sailor walk, weaving and swaying and looking like she was going to fall over any minute, as she hurried from her mother to her father and then shyly off to Shannon, who was sitting on the floor trying to get the baby to come closer.

Kate sat next to Ben on the sofa, trying not to say much of anything, letting Shannon find out what she needed to know.

Emily finally got within a foot of Shannon and stood there sucking on her fist, a little unhappy that the whole thing wouldn't go into her mouth, but otherwise just fine. She started blowing out air, against her fist and making an "Ahhhoooo-ahhhooo-ahhooo," sound as she worked the fist back and forth against her mouth, looking very proud of herself at the noise.

"She seems…happy," Shannon said, sounding as though she needed reassurance about that.

"She is, most of the time," Tina said. "Of course, she's teething right now. That's not easy. And she falls a lot, because she's not that steady on her feet. But the doctor says all that's normal for her age. She's so funny. She stays so busy, she wears herself out. She'll be running across the room one minute, and lying down on the floor asleep the next. When she gets tired, she just collapses wherever she is."

Shannon smiled sadly. "She's really cute, too."

Emily grinned, as if she knew they were talking about her. She seemed to enjoy being the center of attention. She patted her own head with her tiny hand, then reached up and patted Shannon's, again thrilled with herself.

"Watch out," her father said. "She pulls hair."

Emily's grin turned diabolical. She was probably thinking about doing just that, then changed her mind, rushed back to her mother's arms and hid her face against her mother's shoulder.

"She gets shy, too," her mother said.

"Does she know about her…other mother?" Shannon asked.

"As much as she can understand at her age," Tina said. "We're not going to hide anything from her, and Wendy, her birth mother, brought her a little present at Christmas and on Emily's birthday. We send pictures back, and sometimes Wendy calls. She's a freshman at Georgia Tech now."

"So, her birth mother still sees her?"

Tina nodded.

"We don't want to make this any harder for her than it already is," Tim said. "She needs to know that Emily's okay and happy and loved."

"I wasn't sure I could do that… Still see the baby every now and then, I mean," Shannon said looking to Ben and Kate.

"A lot of adoptive parents are open to that, if that's what you want," Ben said.

"Maybe. I mean, it would still be hard." She looked to Tim and Tina, needing them to know that.

"It has to be one of the hardest things in the world," Tina said. "I know how much I loved Emily from the first moment I saw her, and even before that, it was like I was in love with the idea of her and everything I wanted her to be and all the times I imagined us having together. So even before I saw her, I loved her, and it wasn't like I had her inside of me for nine months. I think you must love your baby already, and I'm sorry you don't think you're in a position to keep her. But… well, I just want you to know, there are a lot of people like us, who want children desperately, and the only way we can have them is through the generosity of someone like you."

Shannon worked hard to hold back tears. "I thought

it was kind of selfish, wanting to give up a baby. I thought it just meant you weren't willing to take care of it."

"We don't think so," Tina said. "We see her as a gift. A wonderful, amazing gift. I think any adoptive parent would."

"Plus…having her this past year," Tim said. "Well… don't get me wrong. We love her so much I could hardly tell you. But it's not easy. It's a lot more work than we ever realized. I mean, when they're first born, they can't do anything for themselves. They're completely dependent on you. Everything she needs, whether it's something to eat or someone to hold her or someone to provide a roof over her head—all of it has to come from us. She can't really do anything for herself, and it's a very big job, Shannon. I don't know if I could have done it at your age. I didn't know how big a responsibility it was, until she came."

"I know it would be hard," Shannon said.

"And you've lost you mother?" Tina asked.

Shannon nodded. "Last year. But she didn't really raise me. My grandmother did. She's gone, too, now."

"And your father?"

"I didn't see him much when I was growing up. He took me in when my mother died last year, but…he's really upset about the baby. He kicked me out of the house a few weeks ago."

"So you're all alone?" Tina said. "That's awful."

Shannon shrugged, not trusting herself to say anything, then just blurted out, "It would have been nice to have a father…growing up. Well, one who really cared about me and wanted me."

And then the four of them looked as if they felt sorry for her, exactly what she wanted. Pity. She might feel sorry for herself at times, but she sure didn't need anybody else to. She was going to make some smart-ass crack about that, because she'd rather have them mad at her than pitying her.

But then Emily held out her arms to her father, and launched herself at him.

He caught her easily, as if he'd done it a thousand times, and made a growling noise, then put his mouth to the side of her cheek while he did it. She shrieked and twisted away, than came right back to him, throwing her arms around him.

She seemed completely happy in his arms, completely secure, and his look said he adored her.

Yeah, it would have been nice to have a father who loved her.

The following Friday, Kate could not imagine things going better.

It looked as if Shannon was coming around to the idea of putting her baby up for adoption, which Kate was sure would be the best thing for the baby and probably for Shannon, too.

Kate's sisters had moved in together and seemed fine with the arrangement. Kim had gotten a long-term substitute teaching job at the local middle school, working for a teacher on maternity leave with college behind her. Kate's brother, Jax, was happy as could be with his fiancée, Gwen, and Kate climbed out of bed every morning happy and excited to see what the new day would bring.

She hadn't been this happy in years.

She wasn't getting as much done as she should have at work, but the place wasn't falling apart, either, and she wasn't there until all hours of the evening, either. She had something of a life.

Kate finished with a stack of documents on her desk and moved them into another pile, the ready-to-go-out ones. It looked pretty high.

"Gretchen?" she called out through the open door that led to the reception area.

Her assistant appeared instantly. "Yes?"

Kate picked up the stack of documents. "Just wanted to give you these."

"Oh. Okay." Gretchen took them, but didn't turn around to leave.

"Anything wrong?" Kate asked.

"Well…you're humming," she said, as if it were a crime.

"I am?"

Gretchen nodded. "You've been humming a lot lately."

"So? Is it a problem?"

"No, it's just… Is this some strange kind of coping mechanism, to help you get over losing Joe? Did you read some weird article about humming yourself happy or something? Mind over matter. Something like that? Because that would be like you."

"No, I didn't read any articles. This is not a mind-adjustment exercise." Kate laughed. Would she really have done that? Mind-adjustment exercises? Sure she could hum her way to happiness? She supposed she would have. Gretchen must have thought she was nuts. "I'm just happy, really."

Gretchen seemed puzzled by the concept. "Why?"

"It's a guy," Kate confessed. "A really great guy."

"The priest?"

"Yes." Kate grinned broadly. She couldn't help it. If this conversation went on much longer, she might find herself gushing about him, like some high school freshman who'd snagged a date with the captain of the football team or something.

"He's a priest."

"I know, but he's a really great guy."

"He's probably never going to make a lot of money. He probably doesn't even care about money," Gretchen pointed out.

"I know."

"You want a lot of money," Gretchen reminded her.

Kate shrugged. "So?"

"Does that mean you don't now?"

"I don't know. I just want him."

There. She'd said it out loud. How about that?

"Want him? Like…?"

"In every possible way," Kate said.

It just sort of rushed out of her. Gretchen looked as stunned as Kate felt. But now that it was out… She did want him. In every possible way.

Kate grinned like an idiot, then picked up the phone. Ben answered on the first ring, sounding a little rushed and busy, the way she usually sounded.

"Hi," she said. "How do you feel about ice cream?"

"Are we talking flavor preferences or waffle cones versus sugar cones, or the whole philosophical dilemma that comes into play regarding the purity of the product when toppings are added, like nuts and whipped cream?"

"I just want to know if you like it."

"I do."

"And if you'd like to have some right now?"

"I would."

"With me?"

"Even better," he said agreeably.

"Meet me at the ice cream cart in the park in ten minutes?"

"I'm there," he said.

Kate hung up, then stood and grabbed her purse. "I'm running away for a while."

"But…we have all these things to take care of. You have three closings in the next two days."

"Oh well," Kate said, as she strolled out the door.

Falls Park was a short walk from her office, down one street, down the next and then down the pretty stone steps to the park, which ran along the river surrounding the falls.

Kate walked slowly, knowing she'd get there faster than Ben, and wondered how she could have such a gorgeous place so close to where she worked and hardly ever come here. It was practically a sin.

Late October in Georgia meant the leaves were just starting to fall, the trees still full of gorgeous color. The sky was a deep, spectacular blue, the temperature altogether pleasant.

It was without question a beautiful day, and she planned to enjoy it.

She sat on one of the stone walls that lined the walkway and lifted her face to the sun, closing her eyes and enjoying the warmth and the sense of light on her face.

Sometimes she felt she'd been rushing around her whole life, and had just managed to slow down and catch her breath. What had she been thinking for all those years? All the wrong things, it seemed.

She opened her eyes and saw Ben walking toward her. He was wearing a pair of jeans, with the black shirt of a priest, and he'd taken off his collar. Mrs. Ryan would not be happy, but Kate was.

He was long-legged and lean, walked like a man who knew exactly where he was going, and he had eyes only for her. There was a grin on his face, a light about him, a goodness, that Kate just wanted to soak up like a woman who hadn't had so much as a sip of water in years.

Kate stood up and threw her arms around him the minute he got close enough. He caught her, lifted her off her feet and swung her around, kissing her as he finally set her back down on the ground.

"Mrs. Ryan is sure to hear about this," she said.

"I'm sure she will. But remember, she likes me a little bit now. And I think she likes you. I think she can handle a very public kiss in the park."

"And Melanie. I'm sure Melanie will have the whole story by five, at the latest."

"Do you care?"

"No, I don't. In fact, I thought it was time to put a stop to the whole me-and-Joe-reconciling story. I told Melanie a while ago about everything that happened at the café and asked her to spread the news."

"You asked her to tell people?"

"Yes. Why?"

"Did she look…agreeable, or like she wasn't sure what to do?"

"Now that I think about it, she looked a little strange when I invited her to tell everyone."

Ben nodded. "I might have…talked her out of being a gossip."

"No way," Kate said.

"Yeah, I might have. I gave her my whole floating-blob-of-crap argument weeks ago, and she looked frightened."

"'Floating blob of crap'?"

He nodded, trying to look solemn and serious and failing miserably.

"What is the whole floating-blob-of-crap argument?"

"You know...the karma thing. That what you put out into the world always comes back to you, so you'd better be nice to people, or else."

"This is religious philosophy?" she asked.

"To some people, I guess." He shrugged. "I mean, I think there's a lot to be said for being kind to people, for trying not to hurt them, and she hurt you and a lot of other people, just because it amused her or gave her something to do. I just suggested that if I was her and I spent all my time telling stories about other people, I'd be worried."

Kate laughed. "You were trying to intimidate her. For me?"

"I gave it my best shot," he insisted. "And it looks like it worked. She hasn't said anything, right?"

"I don't know," Kate said, and realized she didn't really care.

"Although it is kind of funny. You come right out and invite her to share your news with everyone, and she's too scared to do it."

"If she hears about us here in the park today, she'll really be stumped about what to do." Kate started laughing.

They got ice cream from the cart, from the same man who'd sold her a fudge bar that first day she'd met Shannon, when her life got turned upside down. Kate got an ice cream sandwich, and Ben got a cup of orange sherbet.

They sat on the stone wall, in the bright sunshine, eating and laughing and just happy to be together.

It felt so good, and yet the things Gretchen said were stuck in Kate's head.

"You know, we don't make any sense at all together," she said finally.

"Why not?"

"Because we don't."

"Do things have to always make sense?" he asked, reasonable as could be.

"To me they do."

"Now, I'm going to say something, not to be mean in any way, just something I think is important that you need to consider. You thought you and Joe made perfect sense."

"Okay, you've got me there, but still…there are just so many things where we're so different."

"Yeah. I'm a man. You're a woman. Big difference, but I like it."

"You know what I mean. What about…ambition? I'm very ambitious, and you're… Well—" She didn't want to hurt his feelings, but he was the most laid-back person she'd ever met.

"Kate, think about it. I believe there are people in the world with problems, and I think through the work I do with the church, I can help them. People come to me when their children are dying or their marriage is falling apart. When they're so depressed they're not sure if they want to go on living and I want to be able to help them. Now, if you're looking for someone to climb the corporate ladder and make a ton of money, I tried that, and there were parts of it that I was good at. I just wasn't happy."

She knew. He'd told her about his adventures in big business. He'd been a personnel manager for a huge company in North Carolina. His family, mom, dad and two brothers were still baffled by his decision to join the church.

"If you're looking for someone who's a part of that business world, it's not gonna be me. But don't think it's a lack of ambition or drive to make a difference or to do something important. What else?"

"Money," she said. "How do you feel about money?"

"I like it," he claimed.

"You can't like it. You're a priest!"

"Sure I can. It makes my job a lot easier. We have people who need help, and very often, money helps. They need medicine or food or a place to stay. They need time off from their jobs to take care of their families, or their kids need clothes. Shannon needed to see a doctor. The church never has enough money."

"I don't know if I'll ever have enough of it, either, and I might...love it."

"Why?"

"Because, I just do," she said.

"Come on. You have to do better than that."

"I guess because things were so hard after my father died. My mother had never worked. She had four kids to take care of, and it was a struggle. For years and years she struggled. I used to see her in the kitchen late at night trying to figure out how to pay the bills, and she worried so much."

"And you decided that when you were grown-up, you didn't ever want to worry about money. Because you saw it as a way of protecting yourself from that one problem you thought was so hard for your family growing up."

"I guess so."

"Kate, you don't love the money. You love the sense of control and security you get from having the money. There's a difference," he said. "What else?"

"You know...the whole God, church thing is really not me," she argued.

"It wasn't me, either, not for a long time."

He'd lost two of his best friends in a car accident when Ben was only twenty-six. A year later he'd gone to the seminary, trying to make sense of it all.

"But it's so important to you now," Kate said. "I'm not like that."

He shrugged. "Doesn't mean you'll always feel that way."

"But maybe I will. And that would have to be a problem between us."

"Would it?"

"Of course it would." She took a breath, looked at him. "Wouldn't it?"

"Has it been a problem so far?"

"I don't know. I guess not."

"And it's not a problem right now, so you must be trying to convince yourself it will become one. What do you think God does, Kate? What do you think the church is all about? Because I think we're all about helping people, or we should be. Life is hard, and we don't always understand why. I don't always know the right thing to do, but I don't think we can go wrong in one, simple thing, and that's trying to help each other. So when I see somebody who needs something, I try to fix it, and from everything I've seen of you, you do the exact same thing."

"But I don't do it because of a church or because of God."

"So? You still do it."

"I do it because I always used to think I knew what was right, what people needed, better than they did."

"You're still trying to help, because you care about the people around you, and I think that's what really counts."

She frowned at him. "You're making me sound much nicer than I am."

"You're making the so-called problems between us sound much bigger than they actually are."

"Still—"

"You'd fit right in at our church, if you wanted to be there. Think of it as a big group of people for you to organize. You love organizing. I know you do. Having someone to manage our money would be great. Having someone tell us how to raise more of it for the things we need to do…that would be great."

"So, you're trying to recruit me as a volunteer now?"

"I'm saying we could find things for you to do that you'd enjoy and be really good at. And a challenge… you like a challenge, believe me, our financial situation is always a challenge."

"So…you want me to be your financial director?"

"I want you to be much more than that, and you know it. But you're not ready to admit it to yourself, and I'm trying not to push," he said. "Still, you must be getting ready to hear all this, because you're starting to get scared, and you don't get scared with someone you don't care about. You only get scared about where a relationship is going when you care a lot and you don't want to get hurt. Kate, I'm not going to hurt you."

It was one of the sweetest promises any man had ever made to her and one of the most sincere, and it scared her half to death.

"Try not to worry so much." He kissed her softly. "You could feel safer and happier with me than you ever did before with a nice bank account."

Chapter Thirteen

Kate sat in her living room late that night, trying not to be scared, trying not to come up with a dozen reasons she shouldn't fall completely for Ben.

She thought he was right.

Money was a safety net to her. She was comfortable with it. She understood it. She thought she could control it. She felt safe with it.

Not so, with a man.

She sighed heavily, feeling sorry for herself, and that's how Shannon found her, when she came walking down the hall.

"Oh, hi," she said. "Sorry if I'm in the way."

"You're not. I'm just sitting here thinking. Do you feel all right?"

"Sure. I just need to go to the bathroom every ten minutes or so. I'm almost always hungry or thirsty, but

I get full when I have two bites. And the baby's sitting on my right hip bone and won't get off."

"Sitting on it?"

"Or something. Digging into it. Elbowing it. Kneeing it. I don't know." Shannon gave the spot a little nudge. "Get off!"

Poor thing did look miserable. Her belly seemed to get bigger every day. If she stood sideways, she looked like a stick that had swallowed a basketball.

"Come and sit down. Or lie down on your left side. Maybe gravity alone will take care of the problem," Kate suggested. "And I'll get you something to drink."

Shannon looked like the least bit of kindness might be her undoing. Kate had been warned the last few weeks of pregnancy were not only uncomfortable but likely a very emotional time. She worried she hadn't been nearly supportive enough.

She went into the kitchen while poor Shannon tried to maneuver herself onto her left side on the couch. It wasn't easy. The girl could barely tie her own shoes anymore.

Kate found a glass and a straw, then looked in the refrigerator. "How about some sweet tea?"

"That's fine," Shannon said.

Kate delivered it, then sat on the edge of the cushion, facing Shannon. She didn't have any makeup on, no artificially white face, no blackened lips, and she might have taken out a piercing or two. She looked like a lost little girl.

"It's not going to last forever," Kate said. "The doctor said it just feels like it will, but it won't."

"I know," she said.

"Ben's arranging for us to meet two couples hoping to adopt soon."

"I know." At the moment she sounded resigned to

giving up her baby. Of course, she could change that in the next second.

Poor girl. Her father hadn't called once, at least, not that Ben or Kate had heard about. It didn't seem like there was anyone left who cared about her, except for the two of them and one of her teachers at school.

What was going to happen to her after the baby came? Kate was starting to worry more and more about that.

"You think I have to give this baby up, don't you?" Shannon said. "You don't think I can manage on my own."

"I think it's hard for you to even understand what it takes to raise a child, and I think you still need someone to raise you. You're only fifteen, Shannon."

"I've been taking care of myself for years. It's not like my mother knew what she was doing when she came back, and my father didn't care at all."

"Yes, but taking care of yourself and taking care of a baby are two different things—"

"I'm not stupid," Shannon cried. "I know that."

"It's not about being smart, and it's not about wanting to do a good job. It's having the ability to do it."

"And you don't think I can?"

"I know it was almost too much for my own mother to handle, and she was in her mid-thirties when she was left alone with me and my brother and sisters."

"Yeah. There were four of you."

"And we all helped. My brother's the oldest, and he helped a lot. I did what I could to help with my sisters, and my mother did what she could, and still…it just takes so much. We all needed so much. Not just money, but her time and attention. We needed reassurance. We needed someone to do the laundry and go to the grocery store and cook and make sure we got to school and did our work there. We needed someone to listen to a million problems, to referee a thousand fights, to be so strong and kind and loving. The list goes on and on, and the needs are constant. It never lets up. I don't know how my mother did it, and she was one of the strongest, kindest, most amazing women I've ever known. To do all that, alone, at fifteen…it just seems impossible to me."

"Girls do it."

"They do. They try. But the question is, what do you want for your baby, and what do you want for yourself? I saw you watching Emily with her father, when she snuggled up to him and went to sleep in his arms. I had a father like that for a while. You don't know how important it is until you don't have it anymore. That little girl, she doesn't know what it's like to be without her dad. She thinks all she has to do is reach out her arms, anytime she wants, and he's going to be there. What would you have given, when you were a girl, to have that? What would you give to have it now?"

Kate was crying by the time she was done. So was Shannon.

"It doesn't mean he's always going to be there for her, just because he's there now. Stuff happens. You know that," Shannon argued.

"I do."

"And just because Paul doesn't want me or the baby, that doesn't mean I'm going to be alone for the rest of my life. I'm gonna have someone who loves me someday, somebody who'll stay. I'm gonna have all those things one day."

"I hope you will. But your baby's coming in a few weeks, Shannon. She needs someone who can take care of her and be a parent to her right now. What if you were her, and someone said to her, you can have this life with your birth mother who's not even out of high school or this one, with a mom and a dad. Which would you pick?"

"That's not fair," Shannon said, weeping.

"That's what's happening right now. Your baby can't choose for herself. You're her mother. You have to decide for her. I think you want her to have the kind of home you didn't have when you were growing up, the things you don't have right now."

"I hate this," she said. "I hate it."

"I know."

"You think I'm stupid for even letting myself get pregnant in the first place."

"No, I think you're a fifteen-year-old girl."

"I was just so lonely, and Paul…he was really nice to me at first. He said he loved me, and there hadn't been anyone who loved me in so long. I just wanted someone to love me and to hold me. It felt so good when he just held on to me."

Kate held out her arms to the girl, and Shannon looked as if there was no way she was going to allow herself that kind of comfort from Kate. But her tears kept falling, and finally she let Kate pull her into an embrace.

They held each other for a long time, Shannon frantic, her grip almost painful. The girl felt tiny, all skin and bones, except for the baby, which was a hard, round lump between them. Kate felt the baby kick hard once, then again. Shannon sniffled and tried to dry her tears with the back of her hand as she eased away.

"It's like she thinks it's a game," Shannon said. "Like she's trying to say hello, or something, or make sure I know she's there."

"She? You think it's a girl?"

Shannon nodded. "Sorry. I didn't mean to…you know."

"It's okay."

"Why are you being so nice to me? You don't even like me."

"I've learned to like you," Kate insisted, and she had. How about that? She hadn't called her Ghoul Girl in weeks.

"But…why?"

"I guess I look at you and think, you need a mother, and you don't have one. I know what that's like, too. My mother died six months ago. I really miss her, and I'm not fifteen and pregnant. I guess I think you must need a mother even more than I do, so…I thought I'd do what I could for you."

"Because of that guy you want to impress? The one who could help you with your business?"

"Shannon, I haven't thought of him in weeks."

"Then, because of Ben."

"No, because of you."

Shannon looked as if she didn't believe it. Or maybe she was too scared to believe it, just like Kate was scared to believe in what was happening between her and Ben. They weren't so different, her and this lost girl who found it so difficult to believe someone could truly care about her.

Sometimes Ben thought he could feel trouble coming. Call it intuition or a kind of advanced warning system, but he had it.

Walking through town the following Thursday afternoon, he was on the lookout for a problem, even though everything seemed to be going well.

His phone rang.

Kate.

He braced himself, but found nothing awry with her or Shannon.

"She's fine, saying she still likes the first adoptive couple you found best, Emily's parents."

Tim and Tina hadn't been looking to adopt right now. They'd been doing Ben a favor, letting Shannon see how their first, open adoption had worked out. But they'd turned out to be Shannon's favorite, and when Ben had asked them last week if they would consider taking Shannon's baby, they were thrilled. They really wanted Emily to have a sister, although a brother would be fine, too.

They'd been gearing themselves up to start the whole, long, stressful adoption process again, and they'd never expected it to be that easy. And they'd gone through the whole process of home visits and evaluations so recently with Emily, it looked as if it was going to be easy to get them approved again as adoptive parents quickly.

"But she still hasn't said she'll actually give them the baby?" Ben asked. He'd feel so much better once she did.

"Not yet, but I think she will. She's been really quiet the last few days, thinking everything through, I think."

Ben crossed over Main Street and headed toward the office of a lawyer who handled adoptions. He wanted Shannon to understand exactly what she was signing, if she agreed to an adoption. "So, I won't set anything else up with other couples wanting to adopt, and...I guess we'll just wait and see. Maybe from here she just has to come to terms with it."

"I think that's it."

"Good." One big problem, very nearly solved. "How are you?"

"Fine," she said. "I'm thinking about—and don't say anything, not one thing—but I'm thinking about taking the entire day off tomorrow."

"Gretchen won't know what to do."

"I know. It's really funny to see how outraged she is, every time I blow off work for a while. I suggested she do the same one day, and she started sputtering. I mean, sputtering. Couldn't get out so much as an identifiable syllable. It was great."

"What are you going to do with your day?"

"Take Shannon shopping. She asked me yesterday if it would be okay if she sent something along with the baby to her new parents, like a locket or a quilt or something, and I told her I thought that would be fine. We're going to look for something special."

"Great."

"And maybe see if my hairdresser can strip the black dye out of her hair. Her hair's coming in now, and her natural color is a pretty reddish blond."

"Normal hair, no black leather...I don't know if I'd recognize her," he said.

She'd look like a girl again, which was what she was. Ben rounded the corner in front of the Corner Café and turned toward Fremont Avenue and the lawyer.

Everything really was going well.

He didn't know of anything that wasn't.

And still, he felt something...

"Let's go to dinner tonight," he said, knowing he'd feel better if he saw her. "Just me and you."

"You mean, like a date?"

"Yeah, like that. There hasn't been any decent gossip in town in weeks, and if you and I aren't going to provide it, who will?"

"You're right. It's our duty. We'll do dinner."

She was laughing, happy and thinking of him, he knew, when he ducked into an alley as a shortcut to his two o'clock appointment and saw two people in the shadows against the back of the bank. He stopped in his tracks, thinking there was something familiar about them and not sure if he wanted to know who they were.

They were embracing, maybe having just kissed, and the moment looked emotional and intense, and this wasn't the kind of place where people stole a kiss unless they really didn't want to be seen. Which meant, they probably felt like they shouldn't be doing what they were doing. And if he actually saw them, he might be faced one day with deciding what to do about what he'd seen, and situations like this never turned out well. He really didn't want to know, but before he could get out of there, the man turned around.

It was Joe. He knew because no fewer than a half-dozen people had pointed him out to Ben over the last month or so, maybe thinking they'd get in a fist fight on the street or something.

Okay. That certainly wasn't a disaster. Joe and Kate were done, and he couldn't imagine Kate being hurt by Joe embracing another woman.

Except the man must have said something, because the woman jumped back away from Joe and then turned to look at Ben.

"Ahh, damn," he whispered.

It was Kate's sister.

Kathie.

"What's wrong?" Kate asked.

He'd forgotten he was even on the phone with her.

"Ahh..." he started sputtering, no recognizable sylla-
bles coming out of his mouth for a moment. "Nothing.
I mean, I was just startled. I glanced up and saw something, and I wasn't sure at first what it was."

Kate's sister had a horrified look on her face. She
turned and ran down the alley. Joe looked grim, and he
was walking toward Ben, like a man facing a firing
squad, a man who wanted to say something before anyone blindfolded him and pulled the trigger.

Ben wanted no part of that conversation.

He turned and walked the other way, Kate's voice
in his ear. "Wait a minute. What was it?"

"Just... Kate..." No way was he telling her the truth
like this, over the phone and without even thinking
about how to do it and whether he even had to do it. And
anything else he could say would have to be a lie, which
meant he had to get off the phone. "Look, I've got to
go. The lawyer's schedule's packed today, but he's
working me in, and I can't be late. I'll talk to you later,
okay?"

"Okay. You sure you're all right?"

"I'm fine. I'll see you tonight at seven."

Assuming he'd figured out what to say by then.

Ben hardly heard a word the lawyer said and felt bad
about wasting the man's time. In his head, the whole
time he'd been there, he kept going over his options
where Kate, Joe and Kathie were concerned. He kept
coming back to one inescapable conclusion. If he saw
what he truly thought he saw—which was an intimate
moment between Kate's ex-fiancé and her sister, then
it was likely Kate would find out about it sooner or later
and that she'd be hurt. Even more so, if she found out
Ben had known and not told her.

Which meant he probably should tell her. He could try to get her to calm down and think things through before she said anything to her sister, and maybe it wouldn't be such an awful scene. She loved her sister, he knew, and he'd hate to see this turn into a big rift between them.

So...maybe he could do some good here, by telling her himself.

But it wasn't his secret to tell. He wasn't even sure there was a secret, although Joe had told Kate he was in love with someone else and that it would never work out. Which could mean he'd fallen for Kate's sister. And unless the guy was a total jerk, that would be a miserable spot to be in. It would certainly be a miserable spot for Kate's sister to be in.

He was starting to wish he was Catholic, and they'd both told him about the situation in confession, so he'd be ethically bound to silence.

No such luck for him.

He had to decide what to do on his own.

Kate stared into the mirror, frowning at her own appearance. She wore a pair of dark slacks and a white blouse, and looked kind of...bland, she feared.

"Tell me you're not going to wear that," Shannon said, standing in the doorway, a look of disgust on her face, as she cradled Petunia in her arms and Romeo trotted after her. They were dog-sitting again. "Don't you own anything that doesn't scream middle-aged businesswoman?"

"I'm twenty-seven!" Kate said, as Romeo grinned up at her and swished his tail, obviously fine with her appearance. "That is in no way middle-aged!"

"Well, you dress like you're thirty-seven," she complained.

"Which is still not middle-aged!" She couldn't possibly be ten years from middle age. No way.

"Surely you own something better than that."

Kate frowned. She'd already been through her closet. Maybe she should have taken Shannon up on the idea of the two of them shopping together for clothes. Not that she'd ever take Shannon's advice about what to wear, but there had to be some middle ground, things both Shannon and Kate didn't love but didn't hate, either.

Unfortunately, Kate didn't own anything like that.

"Dressing well for business is an investment in your future," she said, wincing at how prim she sounded.

Shannon giggled. Petunia was squirming and trying to lick her face. "Did you hear that in a dress-for-success seminar?"

"No." She'd decided it all on her own. "People judge you by how you look. There's no getting around that."

"And you look like an old woman, heading off to work, except you're not going to the office. Take your hair down. Put on some makeup—"

"I *am* wearing makeup." She had on lip gloss and face powder, a hint of eye shadow.

"The pants wouldn't be bad," Shannon continued, "with my jacket—"

"I don't wear black leather."

"Why not? We'll put some skimpy, bright-colored top under it—"

"I don't wear skimpy tops."

"Why not? You're not going to work. You're trying to turn on a guy."

"I don't turn—" Kate stopped herself right there.

What if she didn't turn him on?

She wasn't a middle-aged woman about to go close

a loan. She was going out to dinner with a guy, a really great guy. They'd never had an evening alone together. They'd been too busy with Shannon. But now, they were going out, all by themselves, like grown-ups who liked each other.

"I don't own any skimpy tops," she said softly.

"I do." Shannon took off for her own room, Kate and Romeo trailing after her.

"Wait a minute—"

"It'll be fine. Don't panic. All you need is some color and something that clings in all the right places."

She put Petunia down on her bed, and Romeo jumped up with her. They snuggled together like an old married couple and Kate fought the urge to tell them both to get off the bed. Her controlling tendencies still got the better of her at times.

Shannon opened a drawer, dug through a pile of black tops and finally pulled out a pale-peach colored camisole with lace along the bodice and spaghetti straps.

Romeo woofed his approval. He'd want one for Petunia before too long.

"That looks like lingerie," Kate complained.

"Well, it's not."

"It must be. You'd never own it if you planned on wearing it so that that anyone could see, because it's not black," she said. "And I can't go out in public in that."

"Sure you can. Ben will love it, and if you have to, you can keep the jacket on. All anyone will see is a little lace and your neck. How old did you say you are?"

Kate frowned and took the thing. She'd try it on, just to show Shannon how inappropriate it was. She went back into her room and closed the door in Shannon's face. Peeled off her top and her bra, and put on Shannon's thing. Made out of some kind of shiny, stretchy fabric, it clung everywhere, dipped low in front, not obscenely so, just…low.

"No way," she called out through the closed door.

Shannon opened it and barged right in, leather jacket in hand. "Just try it."

It wasn't the heavy, bad-girl jacket she wore all the time. It was smaller, plainer and…well, not really bad-girlish.

Kate slipped it on.

"There you go. Take the belt," Shannon said, holding out a black leather thing with a silver buckle.

"No. It's too much."

"Just try it!"

Kate did, thinking to prove Shannon wrong, and while she put on the belt, Shannon took the pins from Kate's hair.

"Hey!" Kate protested.

But there was something nice about her long, blonde hair against the black jacket. And the jacket did cover up nearly all of the top. All she saw was a long strip of flesh at her neck and the merest hint of curves of her breasts.

"See?" Shannon said.

"Well…I guess it's not bad."

"Not bad! Wait until Ben walks in the door. He'll be begging me to dress you all the time."

Kate stared at herself, thinking she looked years younger. For years she'd been trying to look older because she handled a lot of money for people, and they tended to be more comfortable with someone who looked older than she was. But maybe she didn't have to do that anymore. She wasn't twenty-four and just starting her own business. Maybe she could loosen up a little on the business suits.

"Admit it," Shannon said. "You love it."

"It's different," Kate said.

"You love it. You know you do."

"How about I let you take me shopping and pick out some things for me, if you let me pick out some things for you for after the baby comes?"

Shannon made a face.

"I won't try to dress you like a middle-aged woman, and you won't buy anything that's black or leather. Deal?"

"I don't have any money," Shannon said.

"It's all right. I do. The middle-aged-woman look paid off big for me, and my sisters won't let me take them shopping."

"And we both know why."

"Maybe you could stop dying your hair black," Kate suggested. "And I'll wear mine down sometimes."

"I think you're taking the big sister, little sister thing too far."

"No, I'm not. We could help each other. We are helping each other. It's going really well, don't you think?"

Shannon shrugged and backed away, leaning against the far wall of Kate's bedroom. Anytime Kate got too close, the girl did this, backed away physically and mentally.

"Just think about it," Kate said. "It could be fun."

Kate was struggling to come up with something to gain back the ground she'd lost when the doorbell rang. The dogs took off at a run, ready to greet their visitor.

"Wait here," Shannon said, turning and heading for the door. "I want to see his face when he spots you."

Kate did as she was told, feeling a bit silly and more

than a little nervous. It was a date. A real date, and she didn't want to mess it up.

She heard Shannon talking to Ben, telling him Kate would be right out.

That was her cue.

She glanced at herself one more time, took a breath and felt as if she was blushing all over. She nearly tripped getting out of the bedroom, and then she was standing in the living room in front of Ben.

He'd put on a pair of black jeans and a form-fitting, crew-neck knit shirt in a soft gray color. His dark hair was still damp at the ends, curling a bit, telling her he'd just gotten out of the shower, and he looked tall and lean and very much a man.

Her nerves kicked up a notch higher.

He took a long, slow look at her from head to toe, then back up again, his jaw going tight, gaze narrowing, and then he whistled at her. "Wow."

Romeo came to look, too. He sat in front of her with his tongue hanging out, a silly grin on his face. He really was the biggest flirt.

Kate blushed even harder.

"Told you." Shannon looked delighted and maybe a bit envious and sad, standing there with her hand on her big belly, Petunia dancing at her feet.

"Have you eaten?" Ben asked Shannon.

"I am not going with the two of you," she said. "I'll find something here when my stomach settles down, and I expect you to have her home at a respectable time."

"Yes, ma'am," he said, holding out a hand to Kate.

She took it and went to his side. He leaned down and kissed her cheek, and she caught a whiff of him. He smelled great.

"I'm not waiting up," Shannon said. "Just in case you… Well, in case you're wondering. I'll be asleep in my room, and I'll probably have my headphones on, listening to some music or something. Just in case. And the dogs will be locked up in my room with me."

Kate gave her a look that she hoped would shut the girl up and said, "Lock the door when we leave."

Shannon rolled her eyes dramatically and shut the door behind them.

Ben walked Kate to his car and opened the door for her, but before she could climb inside, he stopped her by catching her hand in his and stepping back and looking at her again.

"Too much?" she asked.

"Not at all. I just wanted to make sure it was you in there."

"Shannon did it."

"I figured."

"She told me I dress like a middle-aged banker."

"Well…I like the skirts. I could like them more if they were a little bit shorter, but I like them."

"Leg man, are you?"

He nodded. "Although the…what is that little thing you're wearing?"

"Underwear, I'm afraid," Kate said, blushing furiously.

"Oh." He grinned even harder, then put his big, warm hands on either side of her waist, beneath the jacket, against the clingy, peach top. He leaned down and kissed the side of her neck. "It's nice. Very nice."

Kate slid into his arms, holding him close and leaned her face up for his kiss. There was something to be said for this grown-up dating thing.

His kiss was slow and very, very thorough. She knew

the taste of him now, the fit of his mouth against hers, his body against hers, the warm, welcome of his arms and little zing that went through her whenever he got this close to her.

It got stronger all the time. It got harder to pull away every, single time. Something inside of her said that this was her place in the world. Hers and no one else's. That she was perfectly safe in his arms.

Need pushed her on. They kissed frantically, hungrily for a long moment, and then backed away from each other, both of them breathing hard.

"I think we need to go now. Two of your neighbors' porch lights just came on. I see faces pressed against the windows across the street."

"Doing your part to liven things up in this town?" she asked.

He shrugged, still grinning. "Somebody has to."

Heads turned as they walked into the restaurant.

Whispers followed them.

Kate didn't care. She was through worrying about what people thought of her every move. Besides, she wanted to be with this man. Nothing was going to stop her.

The hostess led them to a quiet table in the back, and when they sat down, their knees bumped together. He left his there, against hers, then took her hand. She could have just sat there quite happily, not saying or doing anything, just looking at him, him grinning at her.

The waiter arrived. They realized at the same time that they hadn't so much as glanced at the menu. He gave them an indulgent look, then looked surprised.

"Kate Cassidy?" he asked.

She nodded.

"Jax's sister? The oldest one?"

"Yes."

His mouth hung open for a moment before he managed to close it. "You look different."

Should she thank him for that? Kate wasn't sure. Then she realized who he was. "You ran track with my brother? Ryan Wilkins?"

"Yeah."

"Good to see you again."

"You, too," he said, then seemed to realize where he was and what he was supposed to be doing and excused himself to go take care of a couple at another table.

She and Ben went back to gazing at each other and grinning.

So the man was good in a crisis. He was good at taking care of people. He was honest and kind, really cute and a great kisser. She felt safe and beautiful with him, both at the same time.

"What are you thinking?" he asked.

"That I'm really glad I walked into the Big Brothers/Big Sisters office that day."

"Me, too." He leaned over to kiss her when her phone started ringing.

"Sorry. I'm sorry. I'll turn it off." But when she looked down at the number on her Caller ID, it was her own house. Kate answered the phone and said. "Shannon?"

"I think something's wrong," the girl said. "Something with the baby."

Chapter Fourteen

Something was wrong.

The baby was coming.

"What do you mean, the baby's coming?" Kate said forty minutes later, after they'd gotten to Shannon, panicked and called an ambulance, rushed with her to the hospital and had the doctor examine her.

"I mean, the baby's coming."

"It can't come now," Kate said. "It's not due for three weeks."

Shannon didn't say anything. She looked speechless for once in her life.

The doctor, who looked about fifteen himself, looked amused. "You know that due date they give you is just an estimate, right? A best guess? We're not talking an exact science here."

"Well, it should be. We're not ready," Kate complained. "The baby can't come now."

"You want to try to tell the baby that? I know it won't work, but I doubt you'll take my word for it. So you tell the baby, and if you have any luck, let me know. Me, I'm going to have someone find her a bed on the maternity floor, just in case. How about that?"

Kate fumed silently as the doctor left.

Shannon, huddled into as much of a ball as she could manage around her belly, lay on the gurney looking scared to death. "I don't think I like him."

"Neither do I," Kate said, putting a hand on Shannon's bony shoulder. "Does it really hurt?"

Shannon nodded. "It's awful."

She'd been crying already. Kate was panicking, and Ben was outside, because the doctor had wanted to examine Shannon, and that got him out of being in the room. Not for long, because Kate was going to drag him in there. She and Shannon weren't doing this by themselves.

"Okay," Kate said, hating it when someone dared interfere with her timetable. "I guess I just need to have a talk with this baby."

Shannon gave her a funny look. "Did you just make a joke?"

"I don't know. Did I?"

"Because the doctor was joking. He was making fun of you. He was thinking, 'Sure, lady, you just try to tell this baby what to do, but it's not going to listen.' You know that right?"

"I think I was trying to make a joke," Kate said. "I'm a little nervous."

"Oh, great. Now you're scared? Miss I-Can-Handle-Anything? Now you can't?"

"I didn't say that," Kate argued.

Shannon moaned and held her belly. Another contraction was coming. "Get Ben," she cried. "Just get Ben."

Kate did, practically running out of the room and finding him in the hallway, not looking as confident as she'd hoped.

She grabbed him by the arms and said, "Don't you get scared now. Because I'm scared, and Shannon's scared, and you're the only one left to be calm, so you're elected. You're going to be the calm one, the one who copes."

"No, no, no," he said.

"Yes. You got me into this—"

"I did not!"

"You're the one who just had to help her. You're the one who keeps saying everything will work out. We'll, it's time for it to work out," Kate cried. "Now!"

"Okay," he said, taking a breath. "We'll just do it. People have babies all the time, right? Your mother had babies. My mother had babies. How hard can it be?"

He didn't look like he believed it completely, but she appreciated him saying it and being there for her to hold on to. "No getting out of this because you're a man," she said.

"Okay."

Then from the examination room, Shannon yelled, "Ben!"

It was agony.

Sheer agony.

And it went on for what seemed like forever, although the clock told Ben it had only been about seven hours of labor.

He and Kate sat on either side of Shannon, holding

her hand, feeding her ice chips, rubbing her back, breathing with her, counting for her, begging with her, pleading with her, to just hang on and get through this.

Ben decided he'd rather burn in Hell than ever have a baby. He didn't know how anyone did it.

The doctors hadn't wanted to give Shannon any medication at first, because it was too early in her labor, and then all of a sudden, it was too late in her labor.

She'd screamed and cried and seemed more like the child she was than at any time since he'd met her. Poor baby. She was sobbing in her bed, lying on her side with her head buried against her pillow, Kate holding on to her as best she could.

The doctor was gone. The nurses were gone.

And Ben was standing by the window holding her baby, a little girl, born nearly three hours ago. Barely over five pounds and weeks early, but perfectly formed, perfectly healthy.

She was wrapped up in a pink blanket, and she had a silly little pink knit hat on her bald head. She'd come out all splotchy red and wrinkled, but cleaned up beautifully and was now sleeping, as content as she could be in Ben's arms. He swayed back and forth slowly on his feet in a motion that had put her to sleep earlier and gazed down at her now-pink cheeks and her little button nose.

It was a miracle, really, that something so perfect could come out of so much pain and heartbreak for Shannon. She'd been completely overwhelmed by the birth, by how much it hurt and how long it went on, and hadn't so much as looked at the baby.

Ben glanced down into that perfectly innocent face, sleeping so peacefully, oblivious to the turmoil surrounding her and whispered, "Don't worry, sweetheart. We'll figure it all out."

She made a little squeaking sound and stretched for a moment, two tiny fists thrust up into the air and her face scrunching up into a silly frown, before she settled back down and slept some more.

He glanced over to the bed where Kate, tears in her eyes, tried to soothe Shannon, who was sobbing, saying, "I can't do it. I can't do it," over and over again.

Ben walked over to the bed. "Shannon?"

The girl lifted her head just long enough to see the bundle in his arms, then hid her face again. "I told you, take her away. I can't see her. I can't look at her."

He said a quick, silent prayer that he'd know what do say, know the right thing to do, for both Shannon and the baby, then turned to Kate.

"Will you take her?"

"Sure."

Kate stood up, tear tracks on her pale face, and before he did anything else, he leaned down and kissed her softly, then tried his best to hand the baby over to her without disturbing the sleeping infant.

It was harder than it looked, and he wasn't at all sure of how to do it. She was so tiny. Kate finally had her, looking down at the baby as if she was terrified of breaking her. Ben understood the feeling.

"She's tougher than she looks," Ben said, touching the baby's cheek with the back of his hand, then kissing Kate once again.

"Look at us," Kate whispered, going to the door so that Shannon might not hear over her sobs. "Thinking we could handle this. When we had no idea what we were getting ourselves into. What were we thinking?"

"That somebody had to do it."

"And you just stepped forward and did it."

"So did you," he reminded her.

She let out a shaky breath. "I've never felt so inadequate in my whole life."

"But you did it."

"Still...poor Shannon. She was hurting so much, and she needed so much more than any of us could give her. She needed her mother. A real one. Someone who's been with her her whole life and taken care of her and loved her, and instead she gets us. She deserves so much better than that."

"Hey." He put his hand on the side of her face. "We got through it. We got her through it, and look at what's in your arms right now. She's perfect."

One of Kate's tears fell onto the baby's cheek, and Ben wiped it away.

"She is, but what do we do now?"

"Just be here for both of them," he said.

"Be here? That's—"

"Shhhh." He kissed her to silence her. "You're going to wake up the baby."

"I'm terrified of the baby," she confessed. "And Shannon is, too. She wants to give her up right now. She told me so, the last time you went out of the room for the doctor to examine her. She wanted me to go call Tim and Tina right then, to come and take the baby the minute she was born."

"That's what you wanted, for her to give the baby up."

"Yes, but not...not like this. I wanted her to think about it carefully and rationally and make a decision about what's best for her and the baby. This is just because she's exhausted and panicking. Ben, you can't let her do it. Not like this."

"I won't. Promise."

He held open the door for her and then turned back

to Shannon, still huddled into a ball on the bed and sobbing. Ben took the seat Kate had just vacated, pulled up to the side of the bed and put his arms around the girl as best he could, then laid his head on top of hers.

"Oh, Shannon. I'm sorry."

"Did you take her away?"

"Kate took her to the nursery."

"No, you have to really take her away. That couple, the ones with Emily, tell them they can have her, but they have to come get her now."

"Why?"

"Because...I can't do it."

"Do what?"

"Anything. I can't do anything. This was awful. It hurt so much, and I didn't think it would ever be over. I thought I'd die before they got her out of me, and it still hurts all over, and she's...she's—"

"What?"

"I can't do it. I can't take care of her. You were right. I didn't know what I was getting into. It's crazy thinking I could do it. You have to make them take her away!"

"Tomorrow," he said. "If you still feel this way tomorrow, I'll call them."

"No. Today," she insisted.

"Shannon, this isn't something you can do because you're scared right now. This is a decision you're going to have to live with for the rest of your life. You don't want to make it while you're exhausted and upset—"

"I'm not going to change my mind," she claimed.

"Fine. Then there's no reason not to wait until tomorrow."

"I don't want to see her," she cried.

"Why?"

"I just think it'll be easier if I don't have to see her."

"It's not going to be easy, no matter what," he told her.

"Ben, please," she sobbed.

"Okay, I'll tell the nurses not to bring her in unless you ask for her."

"I won't."

"Okay." He was fairly certain she'd change her mind, but there was no sense arguing about it. He put a hand on her head and smoothed down her hair, which was going every which way. She looked as if she was ready to give up on everything, as if she couldn't do one more thing. "How do you feel? Still hurt?"

She nodded.

"Let me get the nurse. She said they could give you something if you were uncomfortable, and then you can sleep."

She grabbed his arm. "Don't leave me!"

"I won't. Either Kate or I will be right here," he promised. "If we're not in the room, we'll be across the hall with the baby."

She nodded, still crying.

"I'll go get the nurse."

Kate was in a small sitting room outside the nursery, one fitted with comfy couches and rocking chairs. The room was empty except for her. The nurses had taken the baby to the baby warmer, something they'd wanted to do right after she was born, but Ben thought it was important to try to get Shannon to see her, maybe to hold her.

Not that they'd had any luck with that.

She heard someone open the door to the room and looked up from her spot on one of the love seats, leaning over the soft, cushioned arm half-asleep, and there was Ben.

She felt as if they'd been through a war together, that had lasted a couple of years at least. Every bone in her body ached. Every one was screaming with exhaustion, and she had a dozen things she needed to do. She'd been trying to make a list of what they'd absolutely have to have, in case Shannon changed her mind and wanted to bring the baby home with her, but Kate felt like she could hardly keep her eyes open.

But she wanted Ben beside her.

He took a seat at her side, put his arm around her, and she leaned into him, wrapping her arms around his waist, her face against his chest.

"How's Shannon?"

"The nurse gave her a shot. She should sleep for a while. I promised we'd stay."

"Of course," Kate said. "The baby's in the warmer for the next hour or so. Does Shannon still want you to call Tim and Tina?"

"I said I would tomorrow, if she still wants me to." He took her piece of paper from her hand. "What's this?"

"A list. Things for the baby, just in case. I can't believe how ill-prepared we were. We don't have anything."

"Kate, you're dead on your feet. The baby has everything she needs right now. This stuff can wait."

"I know, but… You know me. I like lists. I haven't made one in at least a week, and that's so unlike me."

She felt a laugh well up inside of his chest. "What's got you scared now?"

"I'm not scared. I'm just trying to be organized about this—"

"No, you're scared, and I know because the first thing you always do when you're scared is make a list."

"Okay, I'm scared. I'm completely freaked out about what happened in that room. It was so intense. It was nuts. It was like…I don't know. I wasn't sure she was going to get through it, and then I thought, what if she can't? I mean, there's no backing out. You can't turn around and go home. It didn't matter if she wanted to go through with it or not, because she had absolutely no control over it. It was awful!"

There, she'd said it.

It was terrifying.

She could have made a hundred lists when she'd walked out of that room, and not one of them would have helped.

"It was tough," he admitted.

"But you've been through worse?"

"I've sat with parents while their children died. I've officiated at children's funerals. Those are the worst things. In that room with Shannon, it was intense, and it was scary, but it's a miracle, too. There's a brand-new life, and that little girl could be anything. Do anything. The possibilities are endless. And the way she's brand-new and absolutely innocent and pure… She's perfect right now. She's never been hurt. She's never been sad. She's never been disappointed. She's a blank slate, just waiting to be, to live, and that's amazing to me. That's a miracle."

"She is. You're right about that. But poor Shannon. Fifteen years, and she went from being just like her baby, a blank slate, to someone who's lost people she's loved and who've loved her. She's been abandoned by her father and her boyfriend, and now has to face giving up her baby. All that in fifteen years."

"Yeah, it's awful."

"I didn't think it would be this hard for her. Not having the baby...although, that was harder than I imagined, too. But giving the baby up. I mean, she's fifteen. She could very easily be living on the streets right now. She has nearly three years of high school left. There's no way she can take care of a baby. I thought by the time this day came, she'd see that, and it wouldn't be so hard to give the baby up." Kate buried her face against him. "How could I be so stupid as to think it wouldn't be that hard?"

"We all wish things wouldn't be this hard. It's just the way we are," Ben said, stroking her hair. "It's how we get through things, by not knowing ahead of time how hard they're going to be."

"When I was in there, holding her hand while she tried to get through her labor, I kept thinking, she should have her mother. Her mother should be right here with her, taking care of her."

"She had you and me. We didn't do too bad."

"But it's not the same as having a mother." Kate closed her eyes and held on to him more tightly. "And I shouldn't be thinking about me at all, but...I couldn't help it. When I saw Shannon in there, I thought, I'll be doing that someday. I want to get married and have children, and I always thought my mother would be there to hold my hand and help me understand everything I needed to know to be a mother."

"I can't help you with understanding the mothering," he said, dropping a soft kiss on the top of her head. "But I'll be there to hold your hand."

Kate eased away from him very slowly, just enough that she could lift her head and look him in the eye. She was exhausted, but... "What?"

"When you have your children," he said, calm as could be. "You won't be alone. I'll be there with you. I was thinking four would be good, two of each, but after seeing what just went on in that room, well…one might be plenty. We could get through this one more time, don't you think?"

Kate shook her head. Was she actually awake? "You're asking me to have a baby with you?"

"No, I'm asking you to marry me. Although the baby comes along with it. At least, I always assumed it would, and you just said you did, too. So that works, right? We both want the same thing."

"You can't ask me to marry you," she argued.

"Kate, I just did."

She blinked once, then again, took a breath and stared at him. He was still there. "That's it. Just like that? We've known each other for what…a month? Nobody gets married after a month."

"Sure they do. People get married after a great weekend together. Not that I'm advocating that. But five weeks…it's actually been five weeks, and a great five weeks, too. We've been through a lot, and I know what I want. I think I've been in love with you for at least three weeks."

"You're crazy."

"No, I'm not. And I need to point out that in school, I had a good bit of training in psychology. I'm more than qualified to judge, and I'm sure I'm not crazy. Maybe a little nuts about you, but…"

She frowned.

"Okay, bad joke," he said. "I'm nervous. I've never proposed before. Kate, I love you. Please marry me."

"I can't do that."

"Of course you can. You're not engaged anymore,

remember? You're all over Joe, and I know you're scared. The whole thing is scary, but listen to me. *I know.* I'm done. I want you, and I think you know what you want, too."

"No." She shook her head, trying to rearrange the thoughts in her own head or maybe the words he'd said until they made more sense than what she feared he'd said.

"Or you could think about it," he said, looking amused.

He was always laughing about something, and he always seemed to know exactly what she was thinking, to see inside her in a way that no one ever had. It was disconcerting at times, maddening at others, but it was also comforting, reassuring in a way she'd never imagined. She couldn't hide from him, as she so often did with other people, and if he saw inside of her and still wanted to marry her, then it meant he saw her and understood her and still wanted her. Which was sweet. Crazy, but sweet.

"You need help," she said.

"You want me to get a ring and bring flowers and get down on my knees and stuff? Because I can do that. I just…got caught up in the moment, I guess. I hadn't decided exactly how I was going to ask you, and then, when you said that about having babies yourself, I knew I was supposed to be the one beside you, holding your hand, convincing you that you were going to get through it. I knew."

"You can't say things like that." She shook her head. "You and I haven't even had a real date. Shannon had her baby in the middle of our first date. You can't get married without going on a real date. Lots of them. It takes lots of real dates."

"Okay. Just tell me how many. Is there a rule book somewhere? Because I didn't get it."

"And I have things to do," she argued. "I still have to figure out exactly where I went so wrong with Joe—"

"You didn't love him, remember?"

"I have to figure out how I thought I did for so long, when I didn't, so I won't make that mistake again. And then I should probably spend some time alone, you know, getting to know me again, and then…"

"What then?"

"I don't know," she said stupidly. "I made a list weeks ago."

"A list?"

"Yes." It made perfect sense to her. Why didn't he see that? "And I can't marry you now. It's not on my list. Not even close to being on my list."

"So, make a new list," he said. "You'd love that about weddings. They take lots of lists. Lists and lists and lists. You'll be great at it."

"You want me to marry you because it'll give me a chance to make lots of lists?"

He shrugged. "It seemed important to you. The lists, I mean."

"You're nuts," she said, then an odd, almost choking sound came from somewhere near the door.

It was open. Her sister Kathie was standing there, gaping at them.

"Someone told me there was an ambulance at your house last night, and you're not answering your phone," Kathie said. "I had to find out what happened."

"Shannon had her baby, a little girl," Ben said helpfully.

"Oh, I…" Kathie started to back out of the door. "Did he just propose?"

"She doesn't think it counts," he said. "I didn't get down on one knee."

"So…the two of you…?" Again, odd, odd look.

What in the world? Kate said, "Are you all right?"

Kathie nodded. "I just wasn't sure if… Well, actually…" She looked at Ben. "I think I need to talk to you."

"No, you don't," he said.

"I do," she insisted.

"Look," Kate said. "If this is about Joe and whoever he's running around kissing in alleys, it's okay. I know."

"You know?" Kathie asked, looking horrified.

"No, she doesn't," Ben said.

"I do. Melanie Mann called me. She actually sounded concerned about me, and she swears she wasn't going to tell another soul, but she didn't want me to be blind-sided about it, so she told me. Her boyfriend saw Joe kissing someone behind the bank the other day. I don't care. Really, I don't."

Kathie looked miserable, desperate even. There were tears in her eyes.

"Sweetie, what's wrong?" Kate said.

Kathie shook her head, her mouth open, but no words coming out. Finally she looked to Ben and said, "I can't. I just can't. You do it."

Then she turned and fled.

Ben made a face. "People do that to me all the time. They tell me things, and then they want me to break the bad news for them. I don't like that at all."

"Bad news? What bad news?" Kate asked.

"Okay, but first you have to remember that you don't care who Joe's in love with now, right? It doesn't matter to you, because you don't love him anymore, and it's okay if he's happy, right? You wouldn't begrudge him that?"

"No."

"Okay, because this is the hard part. I saw…something the other day. I wasn't sure what, and I wasn't sure what I should do about it, but…the thing is…I think Joe's in love with your sister."

Kate sat there, her mouth hanging open.

Was she really awake?

Because this was getting more bizarre by the minute.

"I know," Ben said. "That wasn't on your list, either."

Chapter Fifteen

Kate got a few hours' sleep, a shower and fresh clothes, then came back to the hospital five hours later to see that Shannon had just woken up, obviously still hurting, but absolutely calm and determined to give up her baby.

She sent Ben home for a few hours, thinking he'd get some rest the way she had, but he said something about shopping for an engagement ring.

Surely he was joking.

If Kate wasn't so exhausted, she'd probably be able to think it through, but right now she was still a mess. Shannon's labor, her beautiful baby girl, Ben proposing, then telling her that her sister and Joe seemed to be in love with each other…it had all been too much for her.

Everything had gone spiraling out of control at a dizzying speed, terrifying her as she hadn't been since her mother died.

She'd slept only because she was exhausted and woken up sure that the entire past twenty-four hours had been a dream.

Except here she was, sitting by Shannon's bedside, the baby across the hall in the nursery, Ben maybe off buying rings, and Kathie probably still weeping.

"Did Ben make the call?" Shannon asked.

"What call?"

"To that couple. Emily's parents. Ben said if I wanted him to today, he'd call."

"Oh, that. You must have convinced him you meant it. He called them and Social Services, to make sure all their preadoption paperwork had been done, and then he called a friend who's a lawyer, who'll draw up the papers. It should all be taken care of by the time the hospital sends you home tomorrow."

"Okay. Good."

"Tim and Tina want to know if it's okay if they come see the baby today?"

"She's gonna be theirs. It's not up to me."

"For now, it is, Shannon. Are you sure you know what you're doing?"

The girl nodded. She still looked exhausted, all pale and tiny, like she'd shrunk in every way, not just her belly. She looked more girlish than Kate had ever seen her.

"You're sure it's the right thing?" Kate pressed.

"Yes."

"How do you know?" Kate had to ask, because it seemed like an enormous, life-altering decision for anyone so young to make, much less to be certain about."

"Because I want her to have everything, and I can't give her anything."

"If it's just money—"

"It's not," Shannon insisted. "I keep thinking about how Emily looked that day we went to visit. How happy she was. Like she wasn't scared of anything, because that was her place, and those were her parents. Did you see how she'd crawl away from them and get so far, and then turn around to make sure they were still there, watching her, to make sure she was okay? And how sometimes she'd get scared and run back to them. And they'd lift her up and hold her and love her, and she'd just grin and lay her little head against them?"

"Yes, but—"

"I don't think I ever felt that way when I was growing up. That safe. Like I had two, sane, responsible, reasonable, strong people looking out for me. I had my grandmother, but she was always sick with something. Nothing really big for a long time, but enough to scare me so bad. Because she was all that I had, and she'd get so tired. She had trouble breathing sometimes, and I'd stay up at night listening, to make sure she was still breathing, because if anything happened to her, I had no idea what would happen to me. I don't remember ever seeing my father when I was little, and my mother would take off and we wouldn't hear from her for years at a time. I couldn't have found her if I'd wanted to. I wouldn't have had any idea where to look. So I never really felt safe."

Tears fell down Shannon's cheeks, and Kate dabbed at them with a tissue.

"It means a lot, to feel safe. To have people who can take care of you."

"It does," Kate said. "But just because your baby would have this couple now, doesn't mean she always would. There are no guarantees. Look at my family. My father died when I was eight."

"But you made it, because you had your mother and your sisters and your brother, and you all stuck together, right?"

"We did."

"So...my little girl will have a sister." Shannon almost smiled. "I always wanted a sister. And I don't know what might happen down the road, but this is the best thing I can give my baby right now, and she needs a home now. You said that. She can't wait for me to graduate from high school or maybe even college and get a job and grow up. She needs it now, and this is what I want her to have."

"Okay," Kate agreed. "I think that is very mature and shows you're thinking things through, and I liked Tim and Tina right away, and I loved the way they were with Emily. When Tina called to check on you and see if you needed anything, she said they've been trying to explain to Emily what's happening, and she just keeps going, 'Ba-bee, ba-bee, ba-bee.' But they keep showing her a doll, trying to explain what the baby will look like, and she might think she's getting a doll instead. I think they'll be very happy together."

"They'd better be."

"You can see her every now and then, you know?"

Shannon nodded.

"I think you should see her now. The social worker said...well, she said it's important." Actually, she wanted Shannon to put the baby into Tina's arms and see the couple with the baby. Something about needing to see them taking care of her baby to understand that she wasn't abandoning her child. "I could go get her and bring her to you now. She's beautiful."

Shannon shook her head. "Maybe when Ben gets back."

"Okay. I'll call Tim and Tina and tell them they can come sometime this afternoon. And we'll wait for Ben."

Shannon started to cry again, not weeping like she was right after she had the baby. Just a slow, seeping of tears from the corners of her eyes. She looked so sad.

"Oh, your teacher called. Betty? She wanted to make sure you were okay. And she wants to come see you, if that's okay?"

Shannon nodded.

"And Charlotte wants to come by, too."

"No. I don't really know her," Shannon said. "I don't guess my dad called?"

"No," Kate said, wishing she could smack the man right now.

"Okay. I didn't really think he would." Shannon absorbed it like a blow. "I just remembered—we didn't get a chance to get something for the baby. Something for me to give to her, to remember me by."

"We can do that later. You're not going to be cut off from her, remember? We'll tell Tim and Tina when they come that you want to send something for the baby. It'll be fine."

"And we didn't get any clothes or anything. She'll need some clothes to wear when they take her. Something pretty."

"Okay. I'll get something. Just tell me what you'd like."

"Something pretty," she said again. "Pink is okay. I used to wear pink. Honest."

"I'll get the prettiest pink thing I can find," Kate promised.

"Okay." Shannon sighed, shifting this way and that in the bed, grimacing as she did. "Don't worry. I'll get out of your house in a few days. I'll find someplace to go. Maybe now that I'm not pregnant, my dad will let me move back in with him."

"Don't worry about that," Kate said. "Not now. We'll work something out."

"No, I know that I have to go, and I will."

Kate wanted to argue, but Shannon seemed exhausted. She couldn't seem to keep her eyes open.

"Why don't you get some sleep," Kate said.

"You won't leave?"

"No, I won't."

Shannon slept, and Kate dozed in the chair beside her bed.

When she woke up, Ben was there, looking all fresh and clean and smelling so good. She got up and went to him as he stood by the door.

"Did you really propose to me?"

"Kate, you were there. You know I did."

"I can't marry you," she argued.

"Sure you can. Try it out. Yyyyyeeeessss. You can say it."

Kate laughed in spite of herself. "I can say it."

"I don't believe you. I need to hear it."

"Ben, you can't trick me into saying I'll marry you."

"Come on. Say it. I dare you."

"And you can't get me to do it on a dare, either. This is serious."

"I am serious. This is as serious as I get. Plus, you're way too serious for both of us. We're a perfect balance for each other. You see that. I know you do."

"Okay, so we balance each other out that way. There's a little more than that to marriage."

"Yeah. And I could make a whole list of ways we

make sense, if you wanted, but the bottom line is, you've been happier and felt more alive in the past month with me, than you ever have in your life, right?"

"I…" Oh, no. Kate was afraid he had her there. She hadn't really thought about it that way. She'd been too busy to think, too busy living and having fun. She felt completely, wonderfully alive. She woke up every day, excited about what it might bring. She thought of when she'd see him again, what he'd do, what he'd say, the way he'd make her laugh, the way he saw the world.

"I knew it," he said, triumphant. "I knew it because I feel the same way. We fit each other, Kate. We're great with each other. I love you. Marry me."

He was on one knee by the time he was done, his hands holding hers, looking up into her eyes, and it was like everything inside of her just melted, like she was powerless in the face of how he made her feel.

She was dizzy, and the room was spinning. Her heart was racing, and it was hard to get enough air. She hung on to his hands and didn't want to ever let go, thinking she might take off flying if she weren't hanging on to him.

"I don't…" She sputtered. "What did you do to me?"

"Propose?" He seemed confused.

"No, that little…thing between us. Did you feel that?"

"Feel what?"

"Is the room spinning?"

"Kate, the room's been spinning for me since I met you."

"It doesn't spin for me. I mean…we have to be practical about this. There's so much at stake, so much to consider. It can't be a purely emotional decision."

"I know. I made you a list." He had to stand up to search his pockets until he found a message slip with Mrs. Ryan's handwriting on it, then flipped it over and held it out to her. "All done."

She didn't want to take it, but he shoved it into her hands and let go of it. She either had to take it or let it fall to the ground.

"Go ahead. Read it. It's step-by-step, just the way you like it. All kinds of things to cross off, one by one."

Tears welled up in her eyes. Practical, sensible, careful Kate Cassidy's hands were shaking. She was terrified. Hours ago, when Shannon went into labor and then had her baby, when she decided to give her baby up and Ben had made that ridiculous proposal and then Kathie had found them together and Kate realized her sister was in love with Joe…everything seemed like it was spinning out of control. She'd just wanted to hide in a corner and wait for the storm to end.

This was the part where she always turned and ran, retreated into herself, but this time, Ben wasn't going to let her.

He'd made her a list:

1. Tell Ben you love him.
2. Say you'll marry him.
3. Pick a date.
4. Say your vows.
5. Make babies with him. (Hold his hand while you have them.)
6. Live happily ever after.

"That's it?" she asked. "Just like that? You think it'll be that easy?"

"Nothing worth having ever is, but I'm not afraid of working hard at making a life with you, Kate, and I know you're not afraid of working hard, either. You know, there are all kinds of books on how to stay happily married. You'll love it. You can study them all if you want. I think some of them have check lists. It'll be great. Same thing with having kids. Lots of lists. You'll be perfect at it."

"I am so far from perfect," she said, crying in earnest and completely unable to stop.

"So am I."

"And…I was with Joe for five years and didn't marry him. Five years. We've been together for five weeks!"

"Okay, I have to say right now, I'm not waiting five years. I know there's supposed to be give and take on things like this, but I'll just have to owe you one. You have to let me win on this. No five years."

"Five months?" she said, her voice sounding odd and strained, kind of like a squeak.

"Wouldn't be my first choice, either. How about five more weeks?"

"You can't plan a wedding in five weeks," she insisted.

"Hey, I've married tons of people. I assure you, it doesn't take nearly as much fanfare as most people insist on. We just need you and me and another minister and our families, probably some people from my church, Charlotte and her husband, Melanie, Betty, Shannon, the baby and her new family…anybody else just have to be there?"

"I guess not," Kate said.

"Okay. Five weeks. Deal?"

"I…uhhh… Youuuuu—"

"Come on. Say it."

"Ben—"

"Wait! I forgot something. Something really important. I've been thinking about this off and on for a while, that if things worked out between us…" He took the list from Kate's hand and added something, drawing an arrow and moving it up on his list, bumping everything else down. "Here."

She looked at what he'd done.

Felt her heart turn over once more, because it was so perfect.

"You think we should keep her?"

He nodded.

"Our own little girl?"

"I couldn't let her go now, and I don't think you could, either."

"I couldn't," she said. "I realized it today. I can't give her up."

"So." He got down on one knee again. "How about it? You'll marry me?"

Kate was going to say yes. She was ninety-nine percent certain she would have, except someone knocked on the door and then just barged into the room without any kind of invitation.

It was the nurse, bringing the baby.

She looked a little oddly at Ben, down on one knee, in front of Kate, at Shannon on the bed, Shannon who was awake now and looked horrified at the sight of the pink bundle in the nurse's arms.

"Sorry," she said. "The adoptive couple is here, and we had instructions to bring the baby to you, sweetheart, and that you'd be introducing them to this little angel. Is that right?"

Shannon shot Kate and Ben a pleading look.

"I'll take it from here," Ben said, on his feet, holding out his arms for the baby.

"She really is an angel. Happiest little thing, and so

pretty and with a beautiful smile. I don't care what any of those silly books say. Newborn babies have gorgeous smiles," the nurse said. "Should I send the couple in now?"

"In a minute," Ben said.

"Okay." She turned to Shannon, her hand on Shannon's arm. "Sweetheart, I want to tell you that one of my son's wives couldn't manage to get pregnant for anything in this world, and some wonderful young woman just like you made them parents six months ago and made me a grandmother, and we make absolute fools of ourselves for that child. We love him so much, he's about to drown in it. Everyone says he's gonna be rotten one day, but we don't care. It's a wonderful thing you're doing, and don't let anybody tell you different."

Shannon started to cry. The nurse did, too.

Once she was gone, Ben walked over to Shannon and put the baby into her arms. Shannon held her like she was made of glass, with love and so much sorrow in her eyes.

Kate stood by her side, gazing down at the baby, and Ben stood by Kate's side, his arm around her, his body strong and steady against hers. He wouldn't let either one of them down, not in all of this.

"She is so pretty," Shannon said.

"A heartbreaker, for sure," Ben said, bending over to kiss her forehead and then Shannon's. He put his palm to the baby's forehead and then to Shannon, whispered a prayer and then smiled down at them. "A little blessing for the two of you. Are you ready to introduce her to her new parents?"

Shannon looked confused, like she'd lost track of what they were doing.

"What is it?" Ben asked.

"I..." She looked from one of them to the other. "But—"

Before she could say anything, a different nurse opened up the door. "Look who I found in the hallway? They can't wait to come inside."

She stepped back and held the door open wide.

Tim and Tina were waiting, big grins and tears on their faces. "Is it all right? Can we come in now?"

Kate let them in, thinking she probably couldn't keep them out at this point. Soon, the four of them were gathered around the bed. There were more tears, more expressions of awe at the baby's extraordinary beauty and her ability to sleep through the commotion they all made.

It wasn't until Kate looked from the baby to Shannon's face that she knew something was wrong.

"Why did you do that?" Shannon asked. "Why didn't you tell them?"

"Tell them what?" Kate asked.

"About the baby? I woke up while you and Ben were talking. I heard him trying to convince you to marry him, and then I heard the two of you say you wanted to keep the baby, that you couldn't give her up, and that's okay with me. Really. But you should have told me, and you should have told them before they came in here and saw her. It's not fair to them."

To her right, Tina gasped and her husband grabbed her hand. Ben tried to keep them calm, and Kate turned to Shannon.

"Shannon, we weren't talking about the baby," Kate said.

"No, I heard you. You said, Your own little girl—"

"We were talking about you," Ben told her, leaving the other couple and coming to stand by Kate's side, his arm around her waist. "We can't just let you go. We've gotten attached to you, and I think you've gotten attached to us."

Shannon froze. She didn't bat an eyelash, didn't seem to so much as breathe for a long moment. "Me?"

"Yes, you," Ben said. "You deserve the same kind of family you want for this baby, and before you say it, I know you're going to think that we could keep the baby, too. But you've found a wonderful home for your baby, and now I want you to let us take care of you, the way you want her taken care of. You're still a little girl, Shannon. You deserve to finish high school and go to college, and have someone doing all that stuff fathers and mothers do. We want to do that for you."

She still couldn't seem to speak, and it looked as if she was getting scared, just the way Kate would have.

Leave it to Ben to know just what to say.

"Plus, you know what Kate's wardrobe is like. She needs help, and I loved that outfit you helped her with the other night, when we tried to go to dinner. So, for the sake of her wardrobe alone…you've got to stay with us."

"For her clothes?"

"Well…that and some other things. She hasn't actually said yes to marrying me yet. I was thinking you could help me convince her."

"I don't…I never thought I'd have a family like that," Shannon said.

Everyone in the room, except for the baby, was crying.

"Look, this is simple," Ben said. "All anybody has to do, at this point, is to say yes, and we're done." He turned to Tim and Tina. "Do the two of you want this baby?"

"Yes," they said.

"Kate, do you want to marry me?"

"Yes," she said.

"Shannon? Do you want to be our daughter?"

"Yes."

"There. What was so hard about that?"

Epilogue

They tried to keep the wedding small and simple, but Kate soon saw that Ben's congregation absolutely loved him and were genuinely thrilled he was getting married. There was no way any of them could be left off the guest list. And half the town seemed to want to be there, probably just to see if she'd go through with it and if her sister and Joe were coming and whether anyone would get into a fight with anyone else.

So, they gave in and filled up Ben's church. Kate's mother's pastor was thrilled to be asked to perform the ceremony and made it seem as if her mother was there by talking about how much she loved Kate and all that she wanted for her and all her children.

Kate's brother walked her down the aisle. Her sisters served as attendants, even though Kathie protested. She still felt terribly guilty, no matter how often Kate tried to convince her everything was okay. Kathie had only been nineteen when Kate and Joe met. Apparently, she'd fallen hard for him right away, thinking it was a schoolgirl crush. But it just never went away, and apparently, after their mother died, there'd been some sort of embrace that ended with a kiss. They both still felt too guilty to be seen together, even though the last thing Kate wanted was for them to be miserable. Ben said to give them time, and she hoped he was right.

Shannon and Emily served as flower girls, Emily, was thrilled with her baby sister and truly loved being with Shannon, as well. Tim and Tina had named the baby Mae, after Shannon's beloved grandmother. The couple and the baby were all there. Emily and Shannon were wearing matching princess dresses, as Emily called them. She'd picked them out, and everyone had been shocked when Shannon agreed to wear hers. Her hair had grown out enough that she'd cut off all the black, and she now had very short, golden-blond curls. She looked beautiful, was doing well in school and seemed to be staring at a boy who attended Ben's church. She didn't know it yet, but her adoption papers were working their way through the system. She'd be officially theirs before too long.

And Ben was…well, he was Ben. Steady as a rock, absolutely sure of himself and what they were doing, even if it had only been five weeks since he'd proposed.

His church had turned out to be just like he was, kind and loving and helpful. They'd opened their arms to Kate and drawn her right in. She should have known she'd feel right at home in any place created by Ben.

Marriage to him was going to be an absolute joy.

There'd be tough times, she was sure, but she wasn't scared of them anymore. She knew they could get through anything.

She felt absolutely at peace and very blessed, while they said their vows, and as he slid her wedding ring onto her finger, she lifted her face for his kiss.

The reception at the church hall was packed. When they hadn't been able to find a caterer on such short notice, the ladies of the church had taken over, baking and baking and baking. It turned into a potluck, and everything was delicious.

Kate didn't think she'd ever smiled so much in her whole life, or danced so much or cried so much, she was so happy. She was afraid the party would go on much too long, but Ben would have none of that, grabbing her and announcing to everyone that they'd have to continue without the bride and groom, because he and Kate were leaving. She blushed furiously, and he laughed. Somebody in the back of the room whistled. Then everyone was laughing and hugging them and wishing them well.

"I can't believe you did that," she said, as they pulled away in the car.

"Hey, you're lucky I'm not trying to get you naked in the car. It's been a very long five weeks."

It had been, and they'd chosen to wait for their wedding night to make love. They'd been so busy pulling together the wedding, taking care of Shannon, trying to get the adoption process started for her and trying to reassure Kate's sister that it was okay if she wanted to be with Joe.

But the waiting was over.

"Where are we going?" Kate asked. He'd refused to tell her anything, not wanting her to tell anyone where they were, so that no one could find them.

"Not far."

They drove for less than thirty minutes, ending up

in the mountains at a cabin owned by a friend of his. Nothing around them but trees and sky and a few birds.

"It's fully stocked for the week. We won't have to come outside for anything, unless we want to use the hot tub on the back deck," he said, opening her car door and taking her hand to help her out.

Then he lifted her into his arms and kissed her.

"I'm never sure how guys do this and still manage to unlock the door," he said, when they arrived at the cabin's door. "Maybe I'm just not manly enough."

"Oh, I think you are, but why don't you just hand me the keys and let me unlock it."

He did.

The next thing she knew, they were just inside the threshold. The door closed behind them, and he had her in his arms, pressing her back against the door and kissing her.

"I didn't think we'd ever get here," he muttered against her lips.

"Me, neither."

"No one knows. And no calls. No phone. I meant to search you before I let you inside."

"You can search me if you want," she said.

"And we're not leaving. Not for anything."

"Deal."

He ran his hands up and down her body, a thoroughly satisfied grin on his face. "Not hiding anything are you?"

"Just some really interesting underwear that Shannon helped pick out."

"Black leather? Chains? I just can't see that under this dress."

"No. Her tastes are changing."

"Thank goodness."

Kate was tugging at his tie, unbuttoning his shirt.

He didn't seem to know where to start with her dress.

"If you want me out of it, you're really going to have to work for it," she said. "You wouldn't believe what it took to get me into this."

He turned her around and groaned. There were a ton of tiny buttons.

"You did this just to torment me," he said, starting at her neck and managing to unhook just one, then another.

"I didn't. I swear."

"You did." He laughed, then kissed the bit of her neck he'd uncovered. "And I think you should pay."

"Pay?"

"Like this." One more button, one more soft, lingering kiss.

Kate gasped. He knew her neck was so sensitive. And apparently he intended to take his time getting her out of the dress, button by button, kiss by kiss.

She was begging before he was done, hardly able to stay on her feet. The buttons went all the way down her back. She'd never known her back was as sensitive as her neck. It seemed as if there were nerve endings everywhere. She shivered and squirmed, all to no avail. He held her there in place, refusing to be rushed, and his lips were so soft, so insistent. She wanted them everywhere, all over her, didn't think she'd ever be able to wait as long as it took, until he got to the very last one.

He placed a kiss at the indentation at the bottom of her spine that was nearly her undoing. Her legs buckled, and finally he let her turn around in his arms, her dress falling to her waist. He ripped off his shirt, and finally they were skin to skin, kissing crazily.

"I am not waiting one second longer," she said, undoing his belt, then his pants.

Somehow he scooped her up and carried her into the nearest bedroom, tugged off her dress and then his pants, and then he was on top of her, sliding inside of her.

"Oh, Ben."

He didn't move for the longest time, as they both tried to catch their breaths and remember the moment and try to allow their first time to last. He kissed her softly, sweetly. "Don't move. I swear, if you move it's over."

"I won't."

"You are."

"I'm trying not to. It feels so good."

He started moving ever so slowly, back and forth, just a bit, and the sensation was exquisite. She groaned and bit her lip and tried so hard to wait, but they'd waited so long. She couldn't help it. Just having him inside her, on top of her, his arms wrapped around her, all the heat and joy of him. It was too much.

She kissed him fiercely and started to move beneath him, and then he did, too, and then they both just exploded together.

It was a long time before their breathing slowed. Kate cried, and he held her and wiped away her tears.

"I think I'm going to like being married," she said, wrapped in his arms, hidden away from the world.

"I love it already, and I love you, Mrs. Taylor."

"I love you, too."

* * * * *

Since when did life ever tell you where you were going?

Sometimes you just have to dip your oar into the water and start to paddle.

THE
SUNSHINE
COAST
NEWS

KATE AUSTIN

▼ *Silhouette*®

SPECIAL EDITION™

HE WASN'T THE RIDE-OFF-
INTO-THE-SUNSET TYPE...

T. J. "Cowboy" Whittaker wasn't looking
to be anyone's hero, but when sheltered
city girl Priscilla Richards turned her tear-filled
blue eyes on him and asked if he could help
her uncover the secrets in her past...well,
how could the sexy P.I. say no?

CALL ME COWBOY
by JUDY DUARTE

Available March 2006

**Judy Duarte "pulls the reader
deeply and satisfyingly into
the hearts and minds of
[her] characters."**

—*Romantic Times* BOOKclub

Silhouette

SPECIAL EDITION™

A BACHELOR AT THE WEDDING

by *KATE LITTLE*

March 2006

The oldest—and singlest—of five sisters
in a zany Italian family, Stephanie Rossi
was too down-to-earth to let her boss,
heartthrob hotelier Matt Harding,
sweep her off her feet. Or was she?
She was about to find out—
at her own sister's wedding....

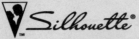

COMING NEXT MONTH

SPECIAL EDITION

#1741 THE BRAVO FAMILY WAY—Christine Rimmer
Bravo Family Ties
Casino owner Fletcher Bravo wanted Cleo Bliss to open her on-site preschools at his resorts, and when they met face-to-face, he wanted Cleo Bliss—*period*. But the last thing this former showgirl needed was a brash, high-living CEO in her life. Would seeing Fletcher's soft spot for his adorable daughter open Cleo's heart to the Bravo family way?

#1742 THE BABY DEAL—Victoria Pade
Family Business
For Delia McRay, hooking up with younger Chicago playboy Andrew Hanson on a Tahitian beach was a fantasy come true. But what happened on the island, didn't stay on the island—for when Hanson Media met with Delia's company months later to land her account, there was a pregnant pause…as Andrew took in the result of their paradise fling.

#1743 CALL ME COWBOY—Judy Duarte
When children's book editor Priscilla Richards uncovered evidence that her father had long ago changed her name, she hired cocksure P.I. "Cowboy" Whittaker to find out why. Soon they discovered the painful truth that her father wasn't the man he claimed to be—and Cowboy rode to the rescue of this prim-and-proper woman's broken heart.

#1744 SHE'S THE ONE—Patricia Kay
Callie's Corner Café
After her credit card company called about suspected identity theft, Susan Pickering turned to police lieutenant Brian Murphy for help. Was Susan's rebellious sister the culprit? Hadn't she turned her life around? As the questions mounted, one thing was certain—identity theft aside, the lieutenant made Susan feel like a whole new woman.

#1745 LUKE'S PROPOSAL—Lois Faye Dyer
The McClouds of Montana
Bad blood between the McClouds and Kerrigans went back to the 1920s. But when Rachel Kerrigan sought Lucas McCloud's help to save her family's ranch, he thought of their fleeting high school kiss and agreed. In return, she made a promise she couldn't keep. Would her deception renew age-old hatreds…or would a different passion prevail?

#1746 A BACHELOR AT THE WEDDING—Kate Little
The oldest—and singlest—of five sisters in a zany Italian family, Stephanie Rossi had ditched her boring fiancé, and was too grounded and professional to let her heartthrob boss, Matt Harding, step into the breach. But attending her sister's wedding with the rich hotelier seemed harmless—or was Stephanie setting herself up to be swept off her feet?

SSECNM0206